A Finders-Keepers Place

ANN HAYWOOD LEAL

A Finders-Keepers Place

HENRY HOLT AND COMPANY

NEW YORK

Henry Holt and Company, LLC
Publishers since 1866
175 Fifth Avenue
New York, New York 10010
www.HenryHoltKids.com

Library of Congress Cataloging-in-Publication Data
Leal, Ann Haywood.
A finders-keepers place / Ann Haywood Leal. — 1st ed.
p.   cm.
Summary: As their mother's manic-depression grows worse,
eleven-year-old Esther and her sister Ruth visit various churches
hoping to find their father, a preacher named Ezekiel
who left them seven years before in 1966.
ISBN 978-0-8050-8882-3
[1. Sisters—Fiction.   2. Manic-depressive illness—Fiction.
3. Mental illness—Fiction.   4. Family problems—Fiction.
5. Single-parent families—Fiction.   6. Missing persons—
Fiction.   7. Schools—Fiction.]   I. Title.
PZ7.L46327Fin 2010   [Fic]—dc22   2009050771

First Edition—2010 / Book designed by April Ward
Printed in August 2010 in the United States of America by
R. R. Donnelley & Sons Company, Harrisonburg, Virginia
1   3   5   7   9   10   8   6   4   2

For (in order of appearance)
Jessica, Andy, and Holly

A FINDERS-KEEPERS PLACE

CHAPTER ONE

I KNEW RUTH WAS GONE the second I woke up. When I looked across the room, I could see her bed was just as I'd made it for her yesterday. The way she liked it, with the pink ruffle peeking out from under her polka-dotted quilt and the yellow happy-face pillow leaning up against the headboard.

"Ruth?" I pulled on the knob of our closet door, and the accordion folds caught on something. I reached around the door and felt for a foot or a hand, but all I got was the lid of my Mouse Trap game and my fifth-grade spelling book.

The hallway outside our room seemed too quiet, and it was almost as if I could hear the house breathing. "Ruth?" I opened the linen closet and yanked out the stacks of towels and washcloths. I stood on my tiptoes and felt along the top shelves.

"Where did you get to?" I got a prickly feeling on the backs of my arms, like when I'd fallen behind my class at the field trip to the soda factory.

The living room at the end of the hallway was exactly the way I'd left it when I'd gone to bed. I kicked aside the pile of zigzag gum-wrapper chains I'd been working on and jumped up on the couch to look out the front window. The shovel was still there, next to the hole in a bare patch of grass.

My mouth got dry when I pictured Ruth falling into that hole. For a quick second I saw her with a hurt leg, unable to climb out. But my brain made me remember. That hole was barely deep enough for a chipmunk to fall in.

I knew there was only one place left to look, and I'd really hoped to find her before it came to that. The bottoms of my bare feet were sweaty when I opened the door of Valley's room.

I stood in the doorway. "Valley?" I asked her quietly.

"Valley?" I said it a little louder and hugged myself. No one ever woke up Valley without plenty good reason. "Valley? It's me, Esther."

I went another step closer and took a good look

around, in case Ruth had wandered from our room in the middle of the night to sleep on Valley's floor. Ruth's body had grown only about half an inch to every two of mine, all her life, and it was easy to miss that tiny thing wedged in somewhere.

There was no sign of her, and I knew I had no other choice. I stepped right up close, so my knees were bumping against the side of the bed.

"Mama?" I put my face next to hers, so she could've smelled what I'd had for supper last night if she'd wanted to.

"Valley? You awake?"

I stepped back. She looked dead, but I knew she was heavily into one of her long sleeps. The kind she has when she takes the round yellow pills from the top shelf in the bathroom. When her mind won't slow down, but her body needs to rest.

I thought about tossing some water on her, but she'd be mad as a hornet. So I knelt down and got up close to her again. "I know Ruth was with you last night. I saw her leave in the truck with you." I got so close, she could probably feel the shapes of my words on her cheek. "Please, Valley? I need you to retrace your steps."

But I knew it was useless. When her breath caught short in the back of her throat like that, she wouldn't be up and around for another three or four hours.

My stomach felt both empty and queasy-full at the same time. I couldn't even think where Ruth might have gone. I tried to push aside the picture of her eight-and-a-half-year-old self out all night.

Valley's face was scrunched up and tight around her mouth, the way it got if the anger hadn't quite made its way out of her. When she got really charged up, that fire in her hung around for a while, even in her sleep. I took a giant step backward, out of reach of her balled-up fist, and I knew where Ruth had to be. It was where we always went to wait it out when Valley got her temper on.

I made my way to the coat closet next to the front door, my heart slowing down a bit, because I knew how I'd find her. She'd be all curled up like a cat, bundled in the ratty yellow blanket that Ford had washed out for her from the finders-keepers place.

I felt for the back wall of the closet and pushed Valley's coat sleeve out of the way. The cigarette smell hung on to the material and made my heart pick up again, as if Valley was lighting one up next to me.

"Ruth?" I knocked on the square door and put my finger through the ring, pulling it toward me.

The crawl space was dark, but if I was on the inside, it felt cozy and safe, all backed in there next to Ruth.

I grabbed the flashlight we kept in the corner and flipped on the switch. That's when my heart cranked up to full speed. No Ruth. Not even a shred from her blanket.

I thought about Valley's tight face and I knew I had to find Ruth fast.

I slammed the square door in place and thought about getting my friend Ford to help. But I didn't want to waste any more time.

As I stepped into the kitchen, I slid in a thick puddle. The sticky pinkness smelled familiar, and that was when I saw all the bags. Five grocery sacks sat in the middle of the table, pink liquid oozing out of the corners and making long, thick trails down the cabinets and onto the floor.

I looked into each bag, and they were all the same. Every one of them was filled to the top with half-gallon cartons of strawberry ice cream. Valley's favorite. But it didn't look as if she'd taken even one bite. The bags sat on the table, and Valley had gone to bed without giving them, or anyone else, a second thought.

I wiped a smear of ice cream from the side of my

hand onto one of the bags, and I saw the receipt sticking to the side of one of the cartons. I peeled it away and held it up.

Mark and Pack. Valley had been to the Mark and Pack!

I tiptoed through the sticky mess and pushed my feet into Valley's green step-in slippers, and I was out the door.

The high handlebars of my bike leaned up against the wooden diamond pattern between the front windows of our house. I swung one leg over the silver banana seat and pushed off down the driveway. I could feel my heart beating as I squeezed my handlebars with my thumbs. We both knew better than to go anywhere with Valley when her anger was rising up.

The ice cream dried on my feet, making the fur from the slippers wrap around my ankles like bandages.

Only a few cars were in the Mark and Pack parking lot, so I pedaled right along the middle of the painted-on lines and tossed my bike down next to the front door. My feet stuck to the rubber mat as the automatic door swung open.

I wanted to run in shouting out her name, but I made myself stand real still and listen. All I heard was "Raindrops Keep Falling on My Head." It was the floaty music without words that follows you around in stores. That music was teasing me today, because it was helping to hide Ruth. I didn't hear any crying, but I hoped she was there somewhere. She had to be.

I crisscrossed up and down the aisles and was thinking about how I could get myself into the back room when I caught sight of something down low and to the right.

It was the blue Keds that gave her away. Only one person I knew put Dole banana stickers on the hole they'd worn over their big toe. My head had a fizzy feeling to it when I let out a whole chestful of air. I hadn't even realized I was holding my breath.

She was curled up on the bottom shelf of the toilet-paper aisle, her head resting on a four-pack. And I was willing to bet that no one at the M and P had even noticed her.

She was partly asleep, but one eye was trying to flip open.

Even though it was cold inside the store, sweat trickled down the middle of my back. My whole body relaxed onto the floor in front of the shelf. I couldn't believe I'd actually found her.

"Esther?" She looked as if she was having trouble getting her mouth around my name.

I put my hand out for her, but she scooted herself back an inch or so on the shelf.

I cleared off some four-packs and wedged myself in next to her. "Hey, Ruth."

CHAPTER TWO

"I GOT LEFT." Her voice was hoarse and small.

"Valley get out of sorts?" I put my hand next to hers, but I didn't touch it. Ruth hated to be touched when she was upset.

She shrugged. "I think she might have been out of sorts when we were coming here in the truck. She was using her halfway words. The ones where she starts up with a few sounds and doesn't finish them."

"You even see her leave the store?" I asked.

She shook her head. "I was reading the Archie comic books, and I looked out and the truck was gone." Her voice was slow and careful, as if she was thinking Valley might be able to hear her.

"Valley Page can be like that," I said. "Quick and

stealthy, like a spy. There one second and gone the next."

She nodded and moved a little closer to me.

I brought my feet up in front of me and peeled some green fur away from my heel. I wanted to hug her tight, I was so glad to see her.

"Hold out your arms." I pushed her sleeves up past her elbows so I could see the place where Valley usually left her angry squeeze marks.

Ruth shook my hands off. "The truck got the bruises. I stayed by the door." She screwed her eyes shut tight, as if she was back in the truck. "She kept banging on the dashboard with her coffee mug." She drew short lines in the air with her pointer finger. "It left little dents."

"Why'd you go with her, Ruth?" I picked at the plastic wrapping on a toilet-paper package. "You know better than to get in the truck with her when she's got her temper on."

She shrugged. "You saw her. She wasn't mad when we got in the truck." She narrowed her eyes at me with the blaming look she gets. "You were on your way out, collecting."

I swallowed hard and thought about how Valley's anger tended to grow real fast, without much warning of any kind.

Ruth leaned back on her elbows, the corners of her mouth quivering up in a tiny smile. "We were going to have a party." She closed her eyes as if she was picturing the spread in front of her. "We were getting strawberry ice cream. Everything was going to be pink. Valley was going to make a big strawberry-pink mountain." Her eyes snapped open, and she sat up. "She's not home decorating, is she?"

I shook my head. "She's in bed."

Ruth blinked hard, as if she was trying to push Valley's pink party to the back of her mind.

"Want a hot dog?" She held out a cocktail wiener. "They had free samples." I could see a pile of toothpicks on top of a small stack of comic books beside her.

"No thanks," I said. "You have it. My stomach's not settled down just yet." I thought about Valley, all tucked into her bed like she was, and I got mad and nervous at the same time. "Let's get going."

She slid forward and stood up, staring down at the floor. "What you got Valley's house shoes on for?"

I curled my sticky toes inside the green fur. "It was the first thing I saw." If my feet hadn't been so coated with strawberry stickiness, those slippers would have been real comfortable. My Keds hardly fit anymore. Seemed like ever since I'd turned eleven, my feet had been growing like crazy.

I picked up my bike outside the store and held the high handlebars steady. "Come on." I pointed to the dip in the middle. "I'll ride you."

Ruth's narrow body fit perfectly in that spot. I felt her slowly relax and lean her head back against me as I pedaled across the parking lot and out onto the road.

"Graveyard!" Ruth let go for a quick second to point at the tiny cemetery to the side of the road, and I heard her take in a noisy gulp of air and hold it.

It was kind of tricky to hold my breath and push hard on my bike pedals at the same time, but I made myself do it.

Ruth let out a stream of air as we passed the last fence post. "Did you feel anything?" She gave a little shiver. "You were kind of late sucking in your breath."

"I'm fine." Grandma Page told me and Ruth a while back that if you didn't hold your breath as you went past a cemetery, a spirit would come out and vacuum-hose your air right out of you. "I wish Grandma never told us about it to begin with. This town is so old, it has a cemetery about every block."

Ruth shook her head. "She was just looking out

for us." She lowered her voice so it was low and raspy, exactly like Grandma's, and made sharp jabs in the air with her pointer finger. "'How'd you think I ended up in this filthy, broken-down nursing home? Hmmm, girls?'" Ruth paused and gave a quick hacking Grandma cough. "'Partly because your mother doesn't give a lick about me, but mostly because I let my breath out too fast going past Saint Margaret's cemetery.'"

Ruth could imitate voices so they sounded almost exactly as if the real person was talking.

"Get a good grip on the handlebars." I pressed my arms in. "I'm going up the curb."

She bounced a bit, but Ruth had good balance. Good enough so she could turn and poke me in the stomach with the sharp part of her elbow. "There she is."

"Valley?" I swerved on the sidewalk and almost dumped her to the ground. But then I saw it was Mrs. Selma Korth, giving off that sad puppy look she always had. Only she never gave off the sad as if she was sorry for herself. She was pointing that sad right at me and Ruth.

"Hold on again." I nudged Ruth's back with my forehead. "I'm switching over to the other side of the street." I had to turn my head to the side a bit. Ruth's hair always got a smell to it when she hadn't had a bath in a while.

"There's no sidewalk." The nervous edge was creeping back into Ruth's voice.

I reminded myself to be patient. "It's easier to dodge a car than it is to dodge Mrs. Korth."

Valley had gotten in Selma Korth's line of fire a couple of months ago when Valley forgot to change out of her nightgown before she went for a walk to the five-and-dime. Next thing we knew, Mrs. Korth was at our back door with a hamburger casserole, trying to get inside and have a chat with Valley.

I steered the bike close to the curb and pushed harder on the pedals. "If you ask me, Mrs. Korth is just jealous. She probably doesn't even own a night-gown like Valley's."

Ruth didn't say anything. She was most likely still stewing about being left.

"And even if she had one, it'd never look like it does on Valley. All cotton-candy pink and flowy." I tried to imagine how Valley must have looked to Mrs. Korth as she walked down the sidewalk in her shiny white high heels, the shimmery pink fabric of her nightgown streaming behind her. "Valley said Selma Korth was strictly a high-necked-flannel person."

I'd had to do some quick thinking with Mrs. Korth at my door. "Valley was just in a hurry to get Ruth her medicine," I'd told her. "Ruth has a fever of 103." I'd made Ruth get on the couch with the afghan pulled up past her chin. "Valley couldn't waste her time changing clothes with Ruth as sick as she was," I'd said.

I could still see Mrs. Korth craning her skinny ostrich neck around the door, trying to get a better look at Ruth on the couch.

I slowed down as I turned onto our block. It was hard to keep an eye on the ground when I was riding Ruth on my handlebars. This was supposed to be a finders-keepers day for me. I'd seen something on the trip over. I was so worried about getting to Ruth, my brain might have been making me see things, but when I pedaled Ruth past the Langs' yard, I knew I'd been right. The blue sparkled up at me from the ground, begging me to go back and pick it up.

I steered into our driveway next door and tilted my bike so Ruth could slide off. "Go on inside and get in a quick nap. You couldn't have had much of a night's sleep on the toilet-paper shelf." I wished I could take that last part back as soon as I said it. Ruth didn't need any reminders about being left.

She made her way into the house without looking back at me. Ruth had always been one to hold a grudge. It had gotten handed down to her from the Page part of the family. And it didn't usually make much sense who she picked to fire her angry looks at. It was hardly ever the person who had made her mad to begin with.

I set my bike down on the grass and walked back next door—along the curb, so I wouldn't miss anything. When I spotted the glass, I could see it was already in medium-sized pieces, which would be perfect for my garden. I scooped it all up in the palm of my hand and ran my little finger carefully over the edges. They were so smooth, I would've believed it was sea glass, if there had been any water nearby to speak of.

I went to the far corner of my front yard and pressed down a fresh patch of dirt with the pads of my fingers. Then I poked the pieces of glass into the dirt, one by one, making a design that went up and over like the tip of a wave. I stood back to look at all of it, and I could see it was just right. When the light caught the cobalt-blue glass, it bounced off the windy trail of gold beer-bottle caps I'd found a couple of days ago. Too bad Valley wasn't a drinker, because if I had just seven or eight more, I could arrange the bottle caps in a swirled border.

I turned and headed toward the house. I still needed to mop up Valley's sticky puddles before she woke up. I wanted to put the house back to normal, because when Valley Page walked out of her room, things could go about a dozen different directions.

CHAPTER THREE

I WAS FOLDING THE LAST of my gum wrappers on the living-room floor when I smelled the heavy cigarette smoke making its way to me from Valley's room. As I got to the hallway, I could see Ruth on her belly, trying to peek under the door.

I nudged her with my toe and turned the door-knob slowly.

Valley sat up against the headboard of her bed, lighting a long white cigarette with the stub of her old one.

Cigarette smoke swirled around her face like a heavy fog. She waved her hand backward at me and shielded her eyes. "Close that door. I have a migraine."

"You got work, Valley." I pulled Ruth behind me.

"Temp agency's got you working at the diner today." I held up the drugstore calendar and showed her the October page.

She breathed out a crooked ring of smoke and slid down the headboard, rolling over on her side and knocking a blue tin ashtray to the floor. "It's too bright in here. Shut the door, would you?"

I backed out of the door with Ruth and pulled it shut slowly. I thought about going in again to try to get her up, but I heard the angry click of the lock on the other side.

"Get me the number for the temp agency, Ruth." I headed toward the kitchen. "It's under the Arizona magnet on the refrigerator."

I'd found that magnet in one of my finders-keepers places, out back of the Salvation Army. I kept it in the middle of the refrigerator, a bright orange Arizona sunset. The cold makes Valley sad, so I knew she would love it in Arizona. It stays warm all the time, and everything is shades of red and gold.

Ruth handed me the number and held the magnet over her head. The kitchen ceiling light shone through the thin plastic and made the sun glow. "What else did Mrs. Foley say?"

My teacher had two favorite things to talk about. First was definitely Richard M. Nixon. She must have talked about him at least six times a day, and she always said it like it was one big long name: "OurPresidentoftheUnitedStatesRichardM.Nixon." I didn't much care one way or the other about him, but I loved it when she talked about her other favorite thing. She told us all about the far-off places she'd been.

"Mrs. Foley said the Arizona dirt isn't muddy brown like it is here. Their dirt is colored with the entire red section of the rainbow."

I lifted the phone receiver from the wall next to the refrigerator and waited for the dial tone.

Ruth leaned in close. "You need to make yourself sound older if you pretend to be Valley again." She peeled a Dole banana sticker off the refrigerator handle and stuck it to her forehead. "Last time you sounded like you were about six. Your voice gets all squeaky when you're telling lies."

She wasn't exactly an expert when it came to fibbing either, but I let it go. Her insides were still raw from her adventure with Valley. "It doesn't matter." I hung up the phone. "It's dead. I'm getting no dial tone at all."

Ruth licked at a tiny leftover puddle of strawberry ice cream on the edge of the counter. "Valley used the phone money for a new necklace." Ruth nodded at the avocado-green beads on the window ledge. "It came with peace-sign earrings. Valley said it was a 'must have' for the fall."

I was thinking that our phone was a "must have" for our house, but I didn't say it out loud.

"Grab your bike, Ruth." I swallowed away the rest of the lump that had settled in when she was missing. "We're going to get you that pink party."

We hopped on our bikes and rode as quickly as Ruth's spindly legs would take her.

"Our first stop needs to be the Regal." I leaned forward between my handlebars and let her catch up.

"We going out to eat?" She stood up and pushed a little harder on the pedals.

There was nothing Ruth liked better than restaurant food, and I figured it was just the thing to get her insides healed back up.

I started to put on my brakes as soon as I got a good whiff of the Regal. Valley smelled like it from head to toe every time she worked there. It was the dead-on combination of fried-up bacon and Mr. Clean.

We stopped at a far corner of the parking lot and leaned our bikes against a light pole. "Listen to me, Ruth." I licked my thumb and smoothed her bangs down flat. "You stick close to me and let me do the talking."

She looked over my shoulder and off to the side, like she did when she didn't want to pay attention.

"I mean it, Ruth." I finger-combed the back of her hair. "Not a word. Or no restaurant food for you."

She batted away my hand. "Yeah. Okay."

The diner was noisy and crowded, and I knew the owner wasn't going to be too happy about Valley not showing up. And neither would the temp agency if they found out. I had to make sure that didn't happen.

The bench by the door was full up with people waiting for a lunch table, and the crowd wasn't about to move over so Ruth and I could get past.

I pulled Ruth around the corner of the cigarette machine and watched an old lady fish her false teeth out of a green plastic water glass. I poked Ruth in the side with my elbow. "As soon as that lady gets up, you need to grab the water glass from the table."

The old lady was putting everything from the table into her purse, from the little sugar packets right down to her dirty coffee spoon. I let out a quick breath of air when she left the water glass and went up to the cash register with her bill.

I had to hand it to her: Ruth was quick. She had that water glass on the floor next to the corner of the cigarette machine in nothing flat.

"Close your eyes and hold still." I dipped my finger in the glass and carefully made water droplets trailing down from underneath her bottom eyelashes. "Now rub at your cheeks a little so they look red and blotchy."

I squinted up my eyes and tried to use the shiny silver of the cigarette machine as a mirror. From what I could see, I had made the perfect long tear. It started in the corner of my eye and snaked its way down the side of my nose.

I leaned against Ruth and nudged the green cup under the cigarette machine. "I'm going to find the boss, and you need to stick close to me." I linked my arm through hers. "You have to let me do the talking, like I said, because Valley can't get in trouble. If the boss complains to the temp agency, Valley won't get sent on any more jobs."

Ruth tried to jerk away, but she clamped her lips together hard so they made a tight, thin line.

"It's him." I pointed toward the other side of the lunch counter. "He's definitely the boss."

A man stepped in front of the window where they hand through the orders to the kitchen. His faded red T-shirt rode up in the back, leaving his gray underwear elastic showing above his baggy blue pants.

The stools were all full, so I pulled Ruth around the corner of the counter.

"You can't be back here, kids." The man grabbed a fry from a plate on the counter and ate it all in one bite.

I pressed my toe into the side of Ruth's foot to remind her to get her whimper going. Nobody could beat Ruth at pretend crying.

He stuffed a couple more fries in his mouth. "My food's not that bad, is it?" When he laughed, he spit some potato mush out on the counter.

I wiped at my eye. "Our mother is supposed to work here today. Valley?"

"Oh, yeah." He squirted some ketchup on the side of his plate. "The one from the temp agency."

I nodded. "She had to leave suddenly, because our grandma's real sick. We're all she's got. Valley had to go take care of her."

Ruth sniffed hard. "Our grandma is really sick."

I wiped at my eye again. "We're not sure when our mom will be back."

He looked at the line by the door. "I don't suppose you can wait tables, can you?"

I shook my head and grabbed Ruth before she could say anything else. But he wouldn't have heard her anyway. He was too busy yelling at someone through the kitchen order window.

I usually feel pretty guilty when I lie, but this guy didn't seem to care one way or the other. The thing was, I hadn't told a genuine lie. I truly wasn't sure when Valley would be back with us again. It could be tomorrow. It could be next week.

I steered Ruth over to the side door at the far end of the counter.

"Can I have my pink party now?" Ruth wiped the fake tears off with the edge of her sleeve.

I nodded at the side door. "You go out that way and make sure no one is trying to steal our bikes. I'll be right behind you."

I guess it was right then and there that I knew all of Ruth's and my churchgoing had paid off. I couldn't have had better luck if I'd ordered it up myself.

CHAPTER FOUR

I WASN'T SURE HOW they'd all managed to fit in there to begin with. The mom was headed toward the cash register, but the kids kept pouring out of the booth in a crowded, grubby line. And they were scratching and pawing at one another like wild animals. The last one I kind of knew from school. Gull Garvin had moved in just a few months ago, at the very end of fourth grade. Now I knew why she was always trying to get an invitation to everybody's house.

Gull smoothed down her pixie cut in front so it made boy bangs, and she tucked her shirttails into her pants. One of her little brothers was reaching his hand up inside the cigarette machine, and Gull grabbed him around his middle with her arm and dropped him down behind the mother. I couldn't tell from where I was if the swear came from Gull or her mother, but I'd heard my friend Ford say it before, and it was a pretty bad one.

With all the commotion at the cash register, I figured this was a perfect time to make my move.

It was a good thing for Valley she wasn't there working, because cleaning that mess on Gull's table was at least a two- or three-person job. What wasn't spilled was dribbled in streaky paths.

Except for a couple of milkshakes. And one of them was strawberry. I grabbed the chocolate, too. And I took off out the door and didn't stop until I got to Ruth and our bikes.

Ruth narrowed her eyes at the milkshake glasses and gave me the accusing look she gets, where she flares her nostrils out wide. "I thought we were having restaurant food."

"This is just our appetizer," I said. "This has got more than half of it left. And lucky for you I was quick, because it was all going to get thrown away."

She stuck the tips of her fingers into the strawberry milkshake and smiled.

"Forget Valley and her pink party," I told her. "I've got something even better. It's going to be a pink *day*."

Ruth must have liked what she heard, because

she drank that pink milkshake down in one long slurp.

And the chocolate one was just the way I like it: all melty, with some of the syrup left at the bottom.

I reached for her glass. "Give it here, and I'll go put them back."

I left the empty glasses out in the open, next to the side door, so they'd be sure to see them.

"Let's get moving, Ruth." I swung my leg over my banana seat. "This pink day isn't over yet."

The Burger Barn was only three blocks away, and Ruth was so excited she didn't have any trouble keeping up with me. Especially when we got within smelling distance. Their French-fried onion rings beat out the Regal's anytime. And there wasn't much chance of the Mr. Clean smell mixing in with it, because I had been inside the place and I had never seen much cleaning going on.

Ruth started to steer her bike toward the front entrance, but I waved her around to the back.

"Are we getting cheeseburgers?" She hopped from one foot to the other. We didn't usually get cheeseburgers unless Valley had gotten extra in her check from the temp agency.

I knew why Ruth had her nose wrinkled up like

it was. It smelled like sour milk and rotten eggs back by the Dumpster, where we were.

I pointed my own nose high in the air. "Try to let yourself breathe the fresh cheeseburger smell from inside the building instead."

We pushed both of our bikes around the other side of the Dumpster until they were most of the way hidden from sight. Then I pulled Ruth down beside me so we were squatting on the pavement next to our bikes. "No talking until I say it's okay." I pressed my finger hard against my lips.

That didn't work for very long, because Ruth settled in with her singsong whimper. Then my legs started aching from crouching so low.

I heard a door slam open, and I clamped my hand over Ruth's mouth.

I saw the wide navy-blue sneakers first. As they came closer, I could see they were attached to a brown-and-orange Burger Barn uniform. I waited for the girl to say something, and I tried really quick to think up what I could say back. But her eyes were gazing off over the Dumpster, and she was carrying on an angry conversation with herself. It sounded as if she was reliving an argument she'd had with someone back inside. She was holding a brown plastic tray with a heap of hamburgers bundled in paper wrappers.

"I work ten times as hard as you do," she was saying in a high-pitched voice. "You are lucky to have me here!"

I sucked in a sharp breath. She sounded like Valley when her temper was starting up. Ruth must have been thinking the same thing, because I didn't even have to remind her to stay quiet. Her lips were sealed in a thin, white line.

I sucked in my stomach and pulled my arms in close, trying to make myself as small as possible, but, luckily, the girl turned away from us.

Then I saw a hamburger wrapper fall to the ground. She must have taken a bite, because I could see bits of pickle and lettuce land on the pavement by her feet. Then she tossed what was left back onto the tray and heaved the whole heap over the side of the Dumpster.

She took her time making her way to the building, and I don't think I let my breath out again until I heard the back door bang shut.

"Okay!" I pulled Ruth to her feet. "I'm going to grab as much as I can and toss it out to you."

She held her arms in close to her sides, her palms cupped like a little bowl. "I'm ready."

I found a foothold and hoisted myself up until I was leaning over the edge of the Dumpster. My nose filled with the rancid garbage smell, but the picture of Ruth on that toilet-paper shelf popped back into my mind, and I made myself keep going. She was going to have her pink day. "Hold my feet and don't let go!"

"Stay on the top, Esther." Ruth squeezed my ankles. "That's where the fresh stuff is."

I tried to breathe only through my mouth, and I hung my head and arms down inside, grabbing for as many wrapped-up packages as I could. The fries had fallen too far down, and they were all mixed in with the swampy garbage, so I didn't even bother with them. I was able to reach some burgers, though, which was lucky, because all of the blood had started to rush to my head, and it felt as if it might explode.

"I've got five!" I wiggled my feet so Ruth would pay attention.

"That's good, Esther!" She tapped my foot. "Come on out. That's plenty."

I tossed the burgers to her and dropped down on the outside of the Dumpster. "Put them in your bicycle basket." I grabbed a handlebar of her bike and pulled it over in front of her. The white plastic basket had a strap broken off, and it hung cockeyed. "Just don't go too fast and they won't spill out," I said.

She pushed off from the side of the Dumpster and got a head start. "We going home?"

I pedaled up next to her so she wouldn't miss what I had to say. "You know just as well as I do that Valley's not at home decorating for your pink party. She's still in her bed, and I don't see her getting out anytime soon."

Ruth stared up ahead and sucked her cheeks in hard.

"You better stop thinking about Valley, or you're going to miss this entire pink day I've been arranging for you!"

I wouldn't hurt Ruth for anything, but sometimes a person's plans take some twists and turns. In a not-so-great way.

Chapter Five

IT WAS MY FAVORITE finders-keepers place, and it was the perfect place to eat our cheeseburgers.

"Bring your bike this way." I motioned Ruth over to a worn part of the fence. I pulled down the two wooden slats that covered the opening. Our friend Ford owned the whole vacant lot.

We'd been going there for at least a year, and we hadn't thought it belonged to anyone until about six months ago when we met Ford. He had been out front one day when we got there, nailing those boards up to keep out trespassers. But I knew that didn't mean us, because he'd left the hole a perfect size to roll two bikes through.

And Ford hadn't even said a word when Ruth

and I used one of the best cars in the back of the lot for our own.

That car didn't have any wheels or doors on it, which made it just right for sitting. You could shift back sideways on the seat and your legs could dangle outside, giving you plenty of stretching room.

"I get the front!" Ruth grabbed one of the cheese-burgers and slid herself backward onto the black leather seat.

"Don't eat yet." I grabbed the cheeseburger from her. "I have a surprise."

I went to my cardboard box in the back seat. I had been saving the string of red Christmas lights for something special. "You've got to use your imagination, though, Ruth." I hooked them over a broken windshield wiper and made them dip down in front of where she was sitting. "Red is kind of like pink, and when the sun catches them, they look like they're plugged in."

She tipped her head back and squinted her eyes so they were half closed. "They're just right!"

I sat down in the back seat and opened up two of the burgers. "This one is going to be yours, because it has pink sauce." I handed the first one to her. "We were lucky that the ketchup mixed together with the mayonnaise so nicely."

She took a big bite and chewed fast, the pink sauce dripping down and making a perfect circle on the front of her sweatshirt.

"Mine just has mustard, but that's okay." I smiled up at the lights. "It's your pink day, not mine."

I could tell she meant to say thanks, because she dipped her head down and chewed slower and looked at me for a long time through her eyelashes.

"Don't peel at the tape on Ezekiel." I pushed the back of her seat. "I just taped his picture up there again."

I leaned over Ruth's seat and smoothed the masking tape down on the bottom edge of the picture on the front of the glove compartment. Daddy smiled out at us from our old living-room couch. The one that sat cockeyed now against the garage, in our backyard. Valley didn't keep a lot of Ezekiel things in the house. I was pretty sure that was because she didn't want anything reminding her about him leaving.

"The tape is covering up the top half of his head." Ruth pointed at it.

"You know I couldn't help that," I said. "Daddy's head was partly torn when I found the picture in the garage. So I had to patch that up at the same time."

"We haven't looked for him in a while." Ruth licked at the corner of her hamburger wrapper. "Valley says he's gone." She turned her voice into Valley's. The one with the icy edge to it that makes me step out of her reach. "'Ezekiel's dead to me. And he should be to you, too.'"

I sat back and kicked at her seat. "Well, he's not. You know better than to listen to Valley when she talks like that. That's a flat-out signal that she's getting out of sorts." I shook my head. "Being on a finders-keepers trip for a person takes a lot of time. It can't be done in one afternoon."

Ruth shrugged in her know-it-all way. "Ford says some things should just be left alone."

I put my hand on her shoulder so she'd pay attention. "Ford doesn't know everything, Ruth. And I wish you'd stop acting like he does."

"He's nineteen." She pointed her face away from me like she did when she wanted to have the final word.

"Yeah, well, Valley's a lot older than that, and she can't even get herself out of bed and down to the Regal for a few hours." I chewed on the last mustardy bite of my cheeseburger. "Just because a person's old doesn't mean they've got everything figured out."

The sun seemed to reflect off the shiny patch on Ruth's arm. Right where the very middle of her cast had been. A whole year had gone by since she got it off, but that patch of skin was always reminding me of how long I'd been searching for Ezekiel. An entire year with no results. I definitely needed to come up with a better plan for finding him.

"Your arm hurt, Ruth?" I licked at some mustard on my knuckle. "You look like you're holding it kind of funny."

She shook her head and chewed away happily on her cheeseburger.

Looking at that shiny patch sometimes made the hair on my own arm stand straight up. I had been at school when the whole thing happened, and Ruth was home sick with a cold. Home with Valley. Ruth had said it was an accident. She'd gotten in Valley's way. She'd woken up Valley before Valley had gotten her full sleep in, and the anger hadn't had a chance to boil off her yet.

I reached over and helped Ruth fold the wrapper on her burger so it wouldn't drip all over her.

She tucked her elbows in tightly and took a big noisy bite.

The day that Ruth got the cast we'd been studying timelines at school. So I'd made myself an

Ezekiel timeline in my head. It was actually more of a Valley one.

The thing you had to do when you were making a timeline was to move in reverse. Ezekiel had left long ago when I was four, and when I thought backward about it, I knew that was right around the time Ruth and I started using the crawl space behind the closet. Valley hadn't had that sharp edge about her until Ezekiel left.

I kicked a pointy scrap of metal away from Ruth's foot. It was easy to figure out once I did that timeline. If I could get Ezekiel to come back, he could smooth over the rough parts of Valley. He'd know what to do when Valley got so out of sorts. He wouldn't have to live with us or anything. He could just come around every once in a while, like he used to. And make us toasted-cheese sandwiches. The good kind, where the cheese remembers to stay inside.

Ruth crumpled up her wrapper and handed it to me. "I like this pink party." She hung her head back so she could see the Christmas lights. "Tell me about your birthday party. Ezekiel was there, wasn't he?"

Ever since we'd started looking for him, Ruth was forever asking me to tell her Ezekiel stories. I had to make some of them up, because I had run out of things I remembered.

"Come on, Esther." She bounced on the car seat. "Did Valley send out invitations?"

It was Ruth's favorite story, and I didn't have to make that one up. Not one tiny bit. It was a big, genuine birthday party with cupcakes and a whole table full of neighborhood kids. "Each one of those kids brought me a present," I said. "Even the ones that were from the same family. And Valley sat beside me on the floor when I opened them so she could write down who gave me what."

Ruth made her hand flat like a notepad and pretended to write on it.

I rooted around in the box next to me until I found the handle of my tin collection-bucket. "I see Ford's got some new stuff out here. Soon as you finish that, we're going on a finders-keepers walk around the vacant lot. We can look especially for pink things."

Ford owned an auto-body shop, and sometimes he took old cars as payment. People who didn't know it was somebody else's property sometimes tossed things over the fence. It made Ford mad, but not me. That just left more stuff to find.

Ruth picked up a broken-off side mirror from

the dirt next to our car. "Look at this!" She held it in front of me. "The glass isn't even cracked."

"Good work, Ruth." I ran my finger carefully around it. "This doesn't have any sharp edges, either. It'll be perfect for our room."

Ruth set the mirror carefully in my bucket. "It's way easier to look for things when it's light out."

She was right. It was always the middle of the night when Valley took us on our finders-keepers trips. She'd figured out a long time ago that people tended to set up for their yard sales ahead of time, the night before. So she'd be on the lookout for notices in the newspaper, and we'd go early to beat the crowd.

Ruth stooped down to get a closer look at a piece of squashed green plastic. "And no dogs here."

That was the problem with the night trips. Ruth got bit once, and she'd screamed so loud the lights had gone on in the house. Valley had made us run all the way down the street to the truck, which was hard to do with Ruth's leg bleeding like it was.

I was going to have to make a basket for my bike, because I was seeing piles of things that would be perfect for my new garden at home. Like an entire headlight. I couldn't figure out why someone had thrown it away. I didn't see one scratch. I lifted it carefully with both hands and carried it to my box in the car.

That made me think about the picture Mrs. Foley had shown us at school. It was of a special place out west. Someone had buried a car in the embankment under a bridge so just the front looked out at you. The car was made to look like a giant's head, with headlights for eyes. It would take some time, but I could do something like that in my garden. Big projects were my specialty.

"Help me with this, Ruth." I set my bucket down outside the car and got my body behind the big white refrigerator.

"I don't feel like pushing that today." She was shining her mirror on a piece of paper. "I think this is starting to heat up."

"Leave that alone and come help me." The white refrigerator was on its side, and I bent down to get my shoulder behind it. "Just a few more pushes and I'll have it where I want it."

She put her shoulder next to mine.

"Take a deep breath and give it everything you've got," I said.

The refrigerator made a short, wide track in the dirt toward our car. Only a couple more feet to go.

"Just one more push, please, Ruth? I want to start

making it into a table." I pointed to a broken stool at the side of the car. "If I find some more of those, we'll have a perfect dining-room set!"

Ruth lined her shoulder up with mine and took a long, deep breath. But what came out wasn't air at all.

CHAPTER SIX

I DIDN'T KNOW HOW there could be so much throw-up inside of a person. Especially someone as scrawny as Ruth.

"It had to have been the pink sauce," I said. "Mine just had mustard, and I feel perfectly fine."

Ruth stared me down right in the dead center of my eyes, as if she wanted me to do something, but I had no idea how to make a person stop throwing up.

That made my own forehead bead up when I saw the dribbles of sweat rolling down the edges of her face. "You might need a doctor, Ruth." I looked toward the fence. "Maybe I should go get Ford."

But she clamped on to my arm with both hands, and I knew I wasn't going anywhere.

"You need to point your head away from me, Ruth." I led her toward the car. "Just in case."

I took a green couch cushion from the floor of the car and helped her lean against it on the back seat. "This will make you comfortable. I got the mouse nest out of it a few days ago, and the stuffing is still nice and soft."

I helped her turn herself around so her top half was almost outside. "Just lean your head out as far as you can if you feel like you're going to throw up again."

"Why is Ruth hanging out of the car like that?" Ford stood behind me, a piece of what looked like a car engine tucked under his arm like a football. "It's Saturday. You guys should be out running around doing stupid kid stuff."

He reached into the front pocket of his gray coveralls and turned up his transistor radio. "I love this song."

Valley loved Elton John, too. But Ford did a better job of singing "Rocket Man." He made his arm all straight, moving it up toward the sky like a space-ship, and he knew every single word of the song. Valley did a lot of extra humming, and she made up her own words to fill in the parts she didn't know.

He pointed at Ruth with his rocket hand. "Her face looks kind of white."

"I ate a bad cheeseburger." Ruth sat up halfway and leaned the side of her face against the seat. "The pink part was rotten."

Ford squinted his eyes up at her as if he didn't believe her. "Where'd you get a pink cheeseburger?"

"Burger Barn." Ruth's cheeks were getting a gray tinge to them.

He turned his radio back down. "You should know better than to eat there. I've heard they don't even use real hamburger meat. I've heard they use . . ." But he must have noticed how Ruth was hanging her top half out of the car again, and he stopped himself from saying the rest.

"I'm kind of in the middle of something, but I'll go get the truck. You need to take her home." He nodded toward our bikes. "I'll toss those in the back of the pickup."

Ford did look pretty busy, with his engine parts and everything, but I figured he didn't want any more of Ruth's throw-up in his vacant lot. So I helped her through the fence opening and waited for him to bring the truck around.

Ford's pickup used to be his dad's. But Ford had

gotten all the old dents and scratches out of it, and he'd painted the whole thing a dark red. I wanted to ride in the back, on top of the wheel well, so I could see better, but I knew Ruth didn't need any extra bouncing around.

We climbed up into the cab, and Ford handed me a paper bag. "I was using it for a litter bag, but Ruth is probably going to need it more." He rolled down the top. "Hold it right below her face," he told me.

I wedged Ruth under my arm, and I hoped she wouldn't notice that the bag was from the Mark and Pack.

By the time Ford dropped us off in our driveway, Ruth had stopped sweating so much. I was thinking she might be on the upswing, as Valley liked to say. Until she let go in my old rock garden.

"It's okay," I said. "I was going to remodel that garden anyway." I kicked some dirt over it, in case Mrs. Korth might decide to wander by. "This garden just had regular old rocks in it, and most of them were starting to come loose from all the rain last week."

We went in through the kitchen, and I listened hard for any sign of Valley. I took in a long breath through my nose as I reached for the big soup pot on top of the stove. "I don't smell any fresh cigarettes. Valley must still be asleep." I turned Ruth toward the hallway. "Go get in bed." I held up the pot. "I need to wash this out a little."

The pot still had some of Wednesday's Hamburger Helper on the sides, so I scrubbed at it in the sink with the bathtub scrubber. I hoped and prayed inside my head that Ruth wouldn't need to go to the doctor. Even if I could get Valley out of her room, I wasn't sure she'd be able to keep wide awake long enough to drive us. From the looks of things, it was likely to be one of her three-day sleeps.

Luckily, tomorrow was a church day, and I could do some good hard looking for Ezekiel. That was one thing I'd figured out even without the timeline. He'd have to have a job, wouldn't he? And once a preacher, always a preacher. If we made enough church visits, we'd be bound to run into him sooner or later.

I dried out the soup pot with the bottom of my shirt and made Ruth some hot tea with honey stirred in. Then I put the pot on the floor by her bed and held the tea so she could take a sip. "Drink up, Ruth, and get some rest. We've got church tomorrow."

The house was almost silent. Except for Valley's voice coming down the hall toward me.

She stood at the doorway of her bedroom as if she was planning on starting her day. But her eyes were only partway open. It was like a weight was pulling down each of her eyelids. Her mouth moved as if she wanted to tell me something important, but she tugged a yellow cigarette case from her pocket and turned back toward her room.

"You okay, Valley?" Her hand was loose and relaxed as she held that yellow case, so I took a step toward her.

She sank onto her bed, put her head back down on her pillow, and stared out at the hall. "Could you get a sheet out of the linen closet for me?" She squinted at the window. "It's way too bright in here, and I just need to get some sleep."

I wanted to tell her that she'd already gotten more sleep than Ruth and me put together, but she was back asleep again, hugging that yellow case next to her face like it was a doll.

I doubled up one of my old Cinderella sheets and taped it over her window with masking tape. Because a sleeping Valley was a whole lot easier than an angry one.

CHAPTER SEVEN

"PULL YOUR SKIRT DOWN, Ruth. I can see your knees." I leaned forward and tugged at the bottom of her hem. "What we've got here are the First Methodists. They like all the skin parts covered up."

I pulled at my own hem as much as I could without tearing anything apart.

"It smells funny in here. Kind of like old cheese." Ruth held the turquoise sash from her dress up to her face and pressed her nose flat.

"It smells fine." Eight-year-olds have no sense of smell. "Your smelling's probably still out of whack from the bad cheeseburger." I tugged the sash away from her nose and retied it in back of her waist. "Are you sure your stomach's settled? I don't think the First Methodists will like it if you start throwing up all over their shiny wooden benches."

"It's fine." She patted the middle of her belly. "I had a butter-and-sugar sandwich this morning, and it's staying right where it's supposed to."

"Get moving, then." I nudged her up the aisle. "They're getting ready to start."

A woman stepped in front of us, blocking our way and a good portion of the light around her. The yellow gladiolas on her dress seemed to stretch pretty much across the entire aisle. "Children's church is that way." She pointed toward a door in the back corner.

"My mom says eleven is old enough for regular church." Valley hadn't said anything of the sort, but I had been practicing speaking my mind out loud where adults were concerned. In fact, there'd be no dealing with Valley if she knew where Ruth and I were. As far as I could tell, she hadn't been anywhere near a church since Ezekiel left.

The gladiola lady leaned her head in a bit, as if she might be getting ready to argue, but I raised my eyebrow and stared right at the bridge of her nose. Say anything with authority and people listen right up.

And, sure enough, she stepped out of my way and wedged herself into a seat a couple of rows up.

But just the mention of the children's church set Ruth's hands to opening and closing and caused her breathing to speed up. "Esther?" She grabbed on to my hand and practically squeezed my pinky off. "You're not dropping me off, are you?"

I tried to shake her loose, but she only grabbed harder. "You know I won't do that," I said.

She walked stiff-legged beside me, and she didn't unlock her legs until we were seated in the front pew, where the view was the best.

I leaned forward in my seat and watched straight ahead for the preacher.

"That him over there?" Ruth pointed at a crowd of men in front by the preaching stand.

I squinted my eyes and looked each one of them up and down. "I wish the seats were closer."

"We can't even scoot." Ruth kicked her white patent-leather toe at the side of our pew. "This right here is wood, and it's nailed in solid."

I grabbed her foot. "You're going to scratch up your shoes. Valley will have a fit." Valley had gotten those shoes almost unused at the Salvation Army. "These First Methodists don't like extra noise.

You'd better sit still or I'm dropping you off at the children's church after all."

I knew I shouldn't have said that, but I couldn't help it. She was ruining my concentration.

I watched her go back into her stiff routine, staring straight ahead.

"And don't you be letting loose with any of your hallelujahs in here." I looked across the aisle. "People here don't talk back to the preacher. They won't like it if you do one of your Baptist happy dances."

She didn't answer, but I could tell by her eyes what she was thinking toward me, and it wasn't very Christian.

I leaned as far forward as I could without letting my dress ride up too much in back.

The man standing up front with his left side to me looked like a possibility. I tapped Ruth's arm with the back of my hand and nodded toward him. "What color eyes has he got? The one in the light-tan suit."

She tilted her head to the side. "Can't tell from here."

But then Tan Suit went and sat down next to Gladiola Lady, so that ruled him out. Daddy wasn't just a churchgoer. I'd never actually been to his church, but he was the main preacher. Valley had made that plain and clear.

I held up my wrist so Ruth could see my watch. "These First Methodists are late getting started. You're going to have to pedal faster on the way home. Much faster than on the way here." I looked at the sharp stick-out bones on her ankles. If she pedaled much faster, those little ankles of hers were bound to break right in half. At least her belly was full again. Her stomach hadn't settled down until almost midnight last night.

"There will be no dealing with Valley if we're not there when she wakes up." I tried to figure down to the exact minute when Valley was in one of her black moods.

I wanted to avoid the whole skin-twist thing. Most people had to use two hands to get a good burning twist going, but Valley could do it on your arm with just one hand. Ruth and I had practiced it on each other, but we never could get it to work like Valley did.

"The other guy is sitting down." Ruth nudged me with her elbow.

Only one person stood in front now, and it was the puffed-up man in the tight gray suit. Everything about him was red and puffy. The buttons in front made his suit pull around his belly in three perfect circles. I couldn't begin to see the color of his eyes, because they were set deep back in the puffiness of his face.

Then Ruth said exactly what I was thinking. "Esther?" Her eyes looked wide and a little nervous. "That's not Daddy, is it?"

I shook my head. "I sure hope not." The man up front had a flat shape to his head on top. I closed my eyes and reached to the very back of my mind. All I could see was the picture I'd taped in the car. I had tried my best with the tape, but you could barely even see his haircut in that picture.

Ruth rolled up her church bulletin and aimed it at the preacher, looking at him as if she had a real telescope. "It might be him." She pretended to remember, but she wasn't yet two the last time we saw him.

I shook my head. "I don't think he could have changed that much." I opened the drawstrings of my suede pouch and took out a half stick of gum for Ruth. The note from school was still there next to my gum wrappers. I took it out and unfolded it, slipping it into my hymnbook so Ruth couldn't see it.

She usually left me alone when I gave her gum, but I'd angled my body away from her, so I could feel her pressing up against me, trying to get a look at the note. I quickly folded it into a small, perfect square again and slipped it back in my pouch.

I closed my pouch and turned around.

Behind us sat a lady with tight silver curls. I knew it wasn't polite to look at a person too long, but the lines on her face were just plain interesting. They made me want to look for a while and follow the lines to see where they led. From the way she sat in her spot, I could tell it was her regular seat. She looked comfortable and settled in, like she'd known that spot for a while. So I knew she was a good one to ask.

"That preacher been here for a few years?" I asked her.

"Oh no, honey," the lined woman said. "He's only been here for three months." She leaned in as if she was telling me a good secret. "Came here all the way from Oregon. Word has it he never left his hometown until he came here." She settled back into her spot. "I like my preachers a little more worldly wise if they're going to be telling me what to do with my life."

I turned back to Ruth. "It's not him."

She took a deep breath and shifted forward to get up. But then the organ music started, and it was too late to leave. It looked as if we'd be getting only one church in today after all.

CHAPTER EIGHT

"HEY, ESTHER. I didn't know you were a Methodist." Gull Garvin looked just like a boy, and she didn't mind telling you she liked it that way. She wore a Boy Scout shirt, complete with the red neckerchief and patches.

"There's a lot you don't know about me, Gull." I wondered how those First Methodists felt about her corduroy jeans.

"I've never seen you here before." Gull Garvin was persistent. You had to give her that much. "I was sitting just a little ways down the pew from you, and I thought to myself, *There's Esther Page from my class. What's she doing here?*"

I shot her my mysterious look, where I raised

one eyebrow and made my mouth into a crooked line. It worked on everyone but Valley.

It worked on Gull. She gave up on the church questions and started trying to get an invite to my house.

"You going home after this?" Gull ran her hand over her short, spiky hair, and I knew what was coming next.

"Yeah," Ruth said, "we're—" She forgot about our rule, so I nudged her foot with my toe.

"We have to clean our room," I said. The thing was, I liked Gull. She seemed to be a nice person, and she'd probably be an interesting friend to have, with all those brothers and sisters. But no matter how much I might like her to come over, I'd have to stick by my rule. Having too many people know our business was just asking for more notes like the one I had in my suede pouch.

"Come on now, Ruth." I grabbed her hand. "See you at school, Gull." I picked up my bike from the church lawn and hung the leather strap of my pouch over the handlebars.

Ford was the perfect kind of friend. He didn't have a whole lot of extra time for us, and when we did get a chance to talk to him, he never asked many questions. Most friends ended up wanting something from you. Usually an invitation to your house, or an after-school snack, or a sleepover. All Ford wanted was for you to ask permission before you took something expensive-looking from his vacant lot.

It took Ruth a while to get her pedaling right. The same thing had happened on the way there. The soles of her patent-leather shoes were slick, and they kept slipping forward off the pedals so the front edges of the pedals caught on the back of her ankles.

She finally took a rest from the pedaling and coasted for a bit. "Our rooms are already clean."

I slowed down until she caught up. "Yeah."

"How come you won't let Gull come over?" As usual, Ruth wouldn't let go of it. "I saw her getting in her car at the Regal. She could bring one of her sisters over and we'd have enough to play Sorry."

"We already have enough to play Sorry. All you need is two, and we got that." I motioned for her to start pedaling again.

"The board's got four sides. If we invite Gull and her sister, we got all the sides filled up."

I shook my head. "You know why we can't invite her."

She rested her forearms on her handlebars.

"It's too hard to explain about Valley and her notions." I pedaled harder so I wouldn't have to talk about it anymore. People never understood, and that was when the trouble always started. I thought about Mrs. Korth. "People are nosy by nature, Ruth."

Valley got a new notion in her head about every couple of months or so. She was a good two weeks into her latest one. She had gotten the notion that we should live like we were in old times.

We had been driving to see my grandma at her nursing home in Pennsylvania, and we'd passed some Amish people with their horse and buggy. I had known right then that a notion was coming on, because Valley had gotten that look about her eyes. Like she was seeing something that no one else could catch hold of.

"Those people are so calm and peaceful," Valley had said. "They live without any modern conveniences to trip them up."

After that day, it wasn't a whole lot of time before things at home started disappearing. Things like my plug-in AM/FM radio with the automatic turntable record player that Grandma had given to me when Grandpa died.

Then it was a few things about every other day or so. I would realize it in bits and pieces. Like when

I went to iron Ruth's Sunday-school dress and all that was left was the ironing board.

"This notion doesn't seem to be holding on so much," I said. "I haven't noticed anything missing for about three days now." That's the way it usually worked with her. Valley would go full speed into one of her notions, sometimes even forgetting to sleep. Then it was as if all that missing sleep tiptoed in the back door and crowded the notion right out of the remembering part of her brain.

She'd probably be out of old times and back in regular old 1973 when she came out of her room. But just in case, I needed to remind Ruth about the new hiding place. "Don't forget to move the toaster to the new spot," I said over my shoulder.

She pushed harder on her pedals to catch up with me. "You mean under the back porch?"

I nodded. "In the back right corner, under that piece of plastic tarp. We don't want our things to get wet. Electric stuff doesn't work if it gets water in it."

I had just rescued some of our plug-in appliances, whatever I could pick up and carry myself, from the front curb. Valley had put it all out for trash pickup last Friday.

"Did you hide the electric can opener?" I let out a long breath of air as we turned the corner.

Valley's truck was gone.

Ruth stopped pedaling and put her feet up on the crossbar. "I set it in the corner of my closet, in my old brown pocketbook. The big one with the thick handle."

We coasted over to the curb and stopped in front of Mrs. Lang's house next door.

Ruth rubbed at the back of her ankle. "You think Valley will make us start wearing those long dresses and white bonnets?"

I shook my head. "Valley didn't say anything about us *being* Amish. She just likes the way they live. Without any extras."

Ruth licked the palm of her hand and wiped at her other ankle. "I miss my cartoons."

Lucky for all of us, keeping a horse cost more than our old pickup, or we'd probably have a buggy sitting in our driveway. And Valley was probably going to be real sorry about selling off our television when she woke up. She'd practically given it away to one of the checkout girls at the Mark and Pack. I wasn't big into shopping, but even I knew that five dollars for a television was a good deal. "One dollar for every year we've had it," Valley had said.

"If we have time later, we could ride over to the

Valu-Mart and watch one of their televisions." I wound my gold-speckled bicycle-streamer around my handlebar.

"You sure that puffy preacher wasn't our daddy?" Ruth kicked a tiny rock into the street.

"There's no way he's Daddy," I said. I thought about the couch picture. "Even if he's gained a few pounds, he couldn't have changed *that* much."

"Did you check out his eyes real good?" she asked.

"They were set too far in." I watched how the green and gold flecks in her eyes caught bits of the sun. "I couldn't see much of any color."

"What if we can't find Daddy?" She nudged my suede pouch with her pointer finger so it swung back and forth on the handlebar. "What if we don't *ever* find him?"

"We have to, Ruth." I thought about Ruth all curled up with the toilet paper. And tomorrow would be Monday, so what was bothering me even more right about then was that folded-up note in my pouch.

Once you got a note sent home from school, you had to watch out. Because there was bound to be plenty more to follow.

CHAPTER NINE

WE HAD BARELY TAKEN the last pedal into the driveway when Valley's pickup came pulling up behind us. The tires moved slowly and surely, like Valley herself when she was working up momentum on one of her notions.

Ruth let her bike drop where it was, knocking one of the yellow plastic daisies cockeyed off the white basket on her handlebars. She moved behind me like a cat, getting out of Valley's line of fire. But neither one of us got so much as one of Valley's looks—those glares straight out of the deep-fat fryer that could sizzle the tips of your ears when she focused a good one on you.

Then, just when I thought all that sleep might

have put her in a good mood, Valley stopped short and eyeballed our church clothes up and down.

She shifted the strap of her crocheted pocketbook to her other shoulder and got a good long stare going at the tops of my eyebrows, causing big beads of sweat to bubble up on my forehead. "Woman at the temp agency said she saw you girls lurking around the Presbyterians a few weeks ago."

I looked down and wiped at one eyebrow with the back of my wrist.

"You don't need to be taking in their nonsense," she said. "You girls can get all the religion you need right here." She pointed to the middle of her chest.

"We'll get you some lunch started, Valley." I knew better than to answer her back, and I stepped softly but quickly on Ruth's toe so she would remember not to, either.

"You can get the groceries in first." Valley nodded at the pickup and headed toward the house. "And don't forget the ones under the seat." She went in the side door and let the screen door slam behind her, the smell of old garlic hanging around in the air after she left.

Valley always had the scent of heated-up spaghetti about her, from one of her old notions that had hung on. She'd heard a while back that garlic kept away sickness, so she sprinkled it on almost everything she ate.

Ruth helped boost me up onto the bumper, and I stepped on the trailer-hitch knob and swung my other leg over the back hatch.

Ruth cocked her head to the side and looked up at me. "What was she talking about back there? What's wrong with the Presbyterians?"

I shook my head. "Nothing's wrong with the Presbyterians. And I don't think you ought to be listening to any of Valley's Bible stories. She changes up the words to suit herself."

I handed the bag of groceries down to Ruth and looked her hard in the eyes. "Valley hasn't set foot in a church that I know of since Ezekiel left. But I've been to enough Sunday schools to know that a person can't be changing up Bible stories when it suits them."

She rested the bag on the bumper and nodded.

"Listen, Ruth," I said. "Valley Page can be very convincing. I know that better than anyone. But there are no Roys or Floyds or LuAnns in the Bible. There's Noah and Moses and Jesus. You're a lot better off listening to the Presbyterians or the First Methodists."

I heard a rock skitter across the driveway, and there stood Gull Garvin, tucking in her Boy Scout shirt and tugging at the wispy side hairs of her pixie cut. "I think there might have been a Roy," she said. She was worse than Ruth about not taking no for an answer. She and her rusty old Schwinn were laying claim to my driveway as if they had gotten a real live invitation.

"I told you we couldn't have company, Gull." I jumped down from the pickup and took the bag of groceries from Ruth.

"Oh, I'm not company." She reached into the back pocket of her corduroys. "I just thought you might be needing this." She held up a folded piece of something, and I knew without even opening up my pouch what she'd done.

I felt my breath catch in the back of my throat. "What you got there?" I hoped she hadn't read it, but I knew there was no chance. Gull Garvin lived with seven brothers and sisters. Knowing other people's business was probably plain, pure survival for her.

"You dropped it at the church." She said it weakly, because we both know she'd helped herself to it. She held it up, but when I went to take it, she put it in her pocket. "I figured you'd be needing it, so I came right over."

I motioned for her to follow me.

"Hold on." Ruth opened the pickup and reached under the seat. She took out a bundle wrapped in Valley's sweater.

I steered clear of it and didn't offer to help, because it was most definitely part of the groceries that Valley hadn't paid for.

"What you got stomach medicine out in your garden for?" Gull picked up a bottle of pink Pepto-Bismol from the flat rock in the middle.

I took it from her and wiped the dirt from the bottom of the bottle. "Must've been my friend Ford. He's always leaving one thing or another for us."

Gull wrinkled her nose. "Throw-up medicine's a weird thing to leave for someone."

I held the screen door for Gull and tried to figure out how I was going to grab the note and get rid of her. She seemed to be the type that did what she wanted, no matter what people told her. And she had been so quick back at the church. I hadn't seen her even near my suede pouch.

"Doughnuts!" Ruth had unfolded Valley's

sweater and was licking the powdered sugar off the inside lid of a Hostess box.

Ruth always slurped Valley's stolen food right down. But I got those guilt streaks that mixed in with the food in my stomach, making it sour and spoiled. I figured that meant I had more of our preacher daddy in me than Ruth did.

Valley came into the kitchen, her eyes all sparkly and bright. She kissed Ruth on the top of her head, and I knew that driveway anger had boiled out of her. "I'm redecorating the house!" She looked right past Gull, as if she were a houseplant, and went on with her plans. "I've got some great ideas for this place." She waved toward the hallway and looped her purse over her shoulder. "I think I'll take the doors off the closets and hang some beads." The leather fringe on the bottom of her purse swung back and forth as she drew long strings of beads in the air with her fingers. Valley changed her pocket-books more than Ruth did.

"Will you take my door off, too?" Ruth squinted her eyes up as if she was trying to see the beads hanging in the air in front of Valley.

"I'm going to go to the Mark and Pack and see if they have plastic necklaces. I can cut them apart and tie the long strands myself." Valley made for the kitchen door and slammed it behind her.

And I didn't give her a second thought until Ruth let out one of her screams. It took her a minute to dig into it, but it was a good one. The kind that starts out silent and ends up making you wish you had backed up about two hundred yards.

CHAPTER TEN

THE TALK OF THE MARK AND PACK was what had done it. I knew it for sure.

I made all the muscles in my face relax, and I turned to Gull. "It's just her nerves. Ruth gets on edge from time to time." I had to grab that note from Gull and get her on her way, but Ruth needed me.

I pulled Ruth down on my lap and hugged her tightly. I held her like that as long as I could, until the tops of my legs started falling asleep and I had to slide her onto the chair next to me.

Gull sat down at the table across from us and helped herself to a doughnut. She didn't give Ruth a second glance. She got to work eating the top off the doughnut. "My sister Wren screams at the drop of a hat," she said. "It's usually broccoli or green beans that sets her off."

Ruth gripped the sides of her chair as if she were an Apollo astronaut.

I pried one of her hands loose and held on to it. "No one is dropping you off, Ruth. No one is going to the Mark and Pack."

She pulled her hand away and looped her elbows through the back of the chair. "Valley is. You heard her, too. Valley's going there."

"You call your mama *Valley*?" Gull scratched at the side of her neck.

"It's her name, isn't it?" I turned back to Ruth and wished Gull would just hand over the note and leave.

"Yes, Valley is going there today to pick up a few things," I said. "And the temp agency is sending her there to work, week after next." I put my arm around the back of her chair. "But you're not going there. You're here. Safe. With me."

Gull helped herself to another doughnut. "My mama would whup me good if I called her by her first name." She took a sharp rabbit bite out of the side of her doughnut. "What's a temp agency?"

"It's kind of like working as a substitute teacher." I rubbed Ruth's hand softly and tried to loosen it up. "When someone calls in sick at a job or goes on vacation, their boss calls a temp agency to send someone to work in their place. Valley gets sent on all sorts of jobs. Last year she got sent to my aunt Dode's fortune-telling office. She had to hide under a big table and knock on it when Aunt Dode called up spirits of people's dead relatives."

Gull licked her finger and pressed it onto some loose powdered sugar on the table. "Sounds kind of fun."

I watched her lick the white powder off her finger. "Even though it was my aunt Dode that was the fortune-teller, Valley had to sign a paper beforehand and promise not to give out any secrets." I got a cold, crampy feeling in my stomach, because it seemed like that was what we were always doing with Valley. Keeping her secrets out of sight.

Ruth finally stopped her whimpering and unwrapped her arms from the chair. "I got left." She blurted the rest of it right out. "She left me at the Mark and Pack."

I had to think real quick before Ruth went too far.

Gull wiped at the corners of her mouth with her thumb and looked at me. "You left her at the M and P?"

I shook my head. "It was a misunderstanding."

Then, without warning, Ruth opened her mouth again. "Valley did." She leaned forward as if she hadn't done anything wrong, and licked her doughnut sugar off the table with the tip of her tongue.

"Night before last." I glanced sideways at Ruth. "I don't think she meant to do it. Valley just forgot she'd brought Ruth along." I put my arm around the back of her chair. "I was asleep when Valley got home, so I didn't notice Ruth wasn't there till morning."

"She was gone all night?" Gull looked interested but not worried.

Ruth must've been conjuring up some bad memories, because she let out a quiet whimper.

"Your mama go back and find her, then?" Gull pushed back from the table and tipped on the rear legs of her chair.

I shook my head, knowing that I'd probably said too much already. "I saw some stuff on the counter from the Mark and Pack, so I knew that's where she was."

Gull let her chair down and narrowed her eyes. "You noticed the M and P bags?"

I nodded. "Valley must've felt sick when she got home the other night, because the bags were still up on the counter. She hadn't unloaded them or anything. That's how I knew where to look first."

Ruth was getting a bit pale about the ears, so I wasn't sure if I should go on.

Gull reached around and pulled a Hardy Boys mystery out of her back pocket. She'd gotten the hard cover off it somehow, and what she held up was just the guts of the book—the inside pages, which she'd marked up like crazy.

She must've noticed me watching her, because she turned to the middle and pointed at some scribbling. "I like to take notes in the margins." She flipped to a page in the back. "Yep." She tapped it with her pointer finger. "This is where the Hardy Boys start to crack the case. Just by recognizing an out-of-state license plate and a mysterious stranger. They put two and two together, like you did."

She smiled at me in an admiring way. "Your mama was sick in bed and you looked for clues to help find Ruth."

Ruth sucked in her top lip and nibbled on it. "They don't turn the lights off all the way at night," she said.

Gull nodded. "That's a good thing to remember."

I didn't know why Gull wanted to remember that, but she took out a blue Bic pen with the tail end chewed off and wrote something on the back page of her Hardy Boys book.

I always felt as if I needed to explain Valley to other people. "Valley forgot about having Ruth along because she was off-kilter."

Gull nodded. "My mama gets off-kilter, too, sometimes. She says all the kids give her a big fat headache."

The thing was, being off-kilter probably meant something else entirely for Gull's mama. When it came to Valley Page, I was glad that Gull had no idea.

CHAPTER ELEVEN

I WIPED UP RUTH'S tongue marks from the kitchen table, and Gull followed Ruth and me down the hall to my room. I noticed that Valley's door was hanging by just one of the hinges, and I kicked a screwdriver out of the way.

I didn't even try to pretend Gull hadn't read every single word of that letter, and neither did she. But I had to make sure she didn't tell anyone.

Gull tossed it down onto my bed and shut the door behind her as if she were guarding a secret for President Nixon.

She sat on the floor and smoothed out a spot in the green carpeting next to her. The shag rug grew up like grass over the toes of her blue Keds. She looked at the wall behind Ruth's bed. "You must have gotten in a ton of trouble for all that writing!"

I shrugged. "Valley doesn't mind. Sometimes she comes in here and adds details to our stuff." I nodded toward the wall next to my dresser. "I usually plan out the designs for my garden on my wall. Paper's too small and narrow. If I draw it out over a wide space, I can see what looks good together."

Gull traced her finger along the whiskers of a cat above the foot of Ruth's bed.

"Ruth's more of a doodler," I said. "When she learns how to draw something, she usually makes whole rows of them." I pointed at the long line of kittens she had made last week.

Gull nudged the letter on my bed with her thumb. "My mama got a letter from our old school once, too. Only it was from the town social worker, not the teacher."

I raised my eyebrow, and she took it to mean she should keep talking.

"It was after my brother Creed told his teacher we didn't have enough to eat at home."

Ruth looked Gull up and down hard, as if she was searching out some skin and bones on her.

"Creed wanted seconds from the lunch cart."

Gull shrugged. "Couldn't really blame him. It was hamburger gravy day."

Ruth's shoulders relaxed a bit.

"Creed said they'd been getting chintzy with the whipped potatoes. And he'd only had about a walnut and a half in his Waldorf salad." She glanced up at the note and back at me. "I'm not so sure if that alone would've gotten us a letter. But then there was the thing with the clothes."

That gave me a sick feeling in my stomach. I looked down at my feet and tugged at the toes of my patent-leather church shoes, trying to stretch them out a size or two. Maybe it was our clothes that had gotten us the note home. I needed to pay better attention to things like that.

"Creed and my brother Robin are always challenging each other to some dare or competition," Gull said. "And Creed bet Robin he could wear the same thing to school for a whole month—even the underwear—without Mama catching him."

Ruth leaned in and wrinkled up her nose. "Without washing?"

Gull nodded. "And it also didn't help that they switched clothes. Robin's shirt hung almost to Creed's knees, and you could see part of Robin's belly when he wore Creed's shirt." She sliced the side of her hand across the bottom of her stomach. "The notes started up the day of the hamburger gravy, but it took just one home visit before they stopped coming."

I pulled the bottom of my church dress down over my knees. Maybe I could take off the sash that came with it and sew it around the bottom hem to make it longer. I was pretty good with a needle and thread.

"A home visit?" Ruth sucked in her top lip.

Gull nodded. "Sat right on the davenport." She laughed. "That woman got a good two-hour dose of Layla and Robin and Seth, and she never came back."

She hunched over and made her belly pooch out. "It doesn't take a rocket scientist or even a social worker to see that the three of them have never missed a meal in their lives."

I laughed, trying to push the worry to the outside edges of my mind. I was kind of enjoying hearing about Layla and Robin and Seth, but Valley would be home soon, and I needed to get Gull out of there.

I stood and held the note up. "Well, thanks for stopping by. I appreciate your bringing this." I took half a step back in case she might have been thinking about taking it along with her.

Gull smiled, as if I hadn't realized she'd stolen it out of my pouch to begin with. "I've been meaning to come by for a while. But you're always rushing out of school. You're hard to catch up with."

Then, all of a sudden, her voice got a whole lot quieter than usual. "You didn't laugh." She made her eyes meet up with mine. "On the first day of school, when Reva Mitchell was making fun of my Boy Scout shirt, everyone laughed. Except you."

"There was no need for the laughing," I said, nudging her out of my room. "It was a nice shirt."

She grabbed a book from Ruth's dresser and yanked out the yellow braided-yarn bookmark, then held it in front of Ruth. "Mrs. Gleason let you take this home?"

Ruth focused her eyes over Gull's shoulder and shrugged.

Gull smoothed her hand over the front cover of the book and held it up for me to see. "That's all my sister Wren talked about when we moved here last May. She was so excited to get put in Mrs. Gleason's class, because she was halfway through this book, but the teacher started back at the beginning so Wren could hear it all. Wren said Mrs. Gleason never let any of them touch it." She ran her finger under the title. "This was one of the first copies of *Charlotte's Web* ever made." She handed it to me. "It's supposed to be worth tons of money."

I opened the front cover and read the perfect handwriting inside. *To my darling Katherine. Love, Grandma Trudy.* I could see Ruth out of the corner of my eye. She had completely turned her back to us, and she wasn't talking. "How do you know she didn't just check it out from the library?"

Gull twirled the bookmark in the air and shook her head. "No way, José. Mrs. Gleason taught Wren how to make a yarn bookmark just like this one. And Wren made them all summer. I keep finding them all over the house."

I tried to swallow the big bunch of air that had settled in the back of my throat. "I'll figure out a way to get it back to her."

Gull got her detective look about the eyes. "Maybe we could break into the school in the middle of the night and put it back."

Ruth shifted nervously on the floor when she heard that one. Mentioning night probably made her think about being left.

Gull stood up and straightened her neckerchief. "I gotta go. Mama's paying me fifty cents an hour to watch Wayne while she sorts through her Avon orders. She caught him smoking her cigarettes in the backyard."

Ruth squinched her eyes up at Gull. "I thought Wayne was younger than me."

"Yep." Gull shoved her Hardy Boys book deeper into her back pocket and left.

"Come on." I grabbed the letter with one hand and Ruth with the other. "We got a whole lot of work to do and hardly any time to do it."

I stopped by my door and flipped my bedroom light on and off a couple of times.

"What are you doing?" Ruth squinted up at my overhead light.

"Just checking." I was worried about the electricity. It was the next logical thing for Valley to get rid of. When she came through the kitchen, she seemed as if she'd let go of that notion. But I wasn't going to take any chances, because I couldn't allow Ruth to be in the dark. It would make her too anxious. "C'mon." I motioned for her to follow me back down the hall.

Ruth kept moving her head toward the letter. I folded it carefully on the kitchen table and stuffed it back in my pouch. So far I hadn't given her a chance to read it all the way through. It was best not to get her nerves going.

Ruth nudged my pouch with the back of her hand. "It has Valley's name on it. I saw Valley's name on it."

I could see she wasn't going to stop nagging at me. "And I'm going to give it to Valley." I reached to the bottom of my pouch and felt around for the house key. "Just not quite yet."

I had to find out why the school wanted her to have a meeting with them. I thought about the social worker at Gull's house, and I sure hoped the school wasn't planning on sending someone to sit on our davenport.

My stomach grumbled.

"You want a doughnut, Esther?" Ruth opened the lid of the Hostess box. "There's still some broken pieces left."

I loved sweets as much as Ruth, but I knew that stolen powdered sugar would catch in my throat partway down. "No thanks."

I reached for the paid-for bag on the corner of the table and checked for the receipt at the bottom. Then I pulled out a tub of margarine and a jar of olives and made myself a quick sandwich.

"I don't think they had jars of olives in the old days." Ruth reached for a slice of bread.

I shrugged. "Valley doesn't always think through all the small details when she gets her notions."

Ruth poked at my pouch again. "What does the letter say?"

I put the lid on the olives and opened the refrigerator. The inside of the door was warm.

I shut the door and felt around the back for the plug. "I need you to reach behind for the outlet. My shoulders aren't as skinny as yours."

"What's in the letter?" Ruth wedged herself into the narrow space next to the refrigerator and plugged it in.

I could practically see her heels digging into the kitchen linoleum, so I opened up my pouch and handed her the letter.

She read it slowly, her lips making funny shapes, as if she was trying to get her mouth around each word.

I chewed on my olive-and-margarine sandwich and watched her go up to the beginning and read it again. Finally, she folded it and handed it back to me. "Why does Valley have to go into the school? She was just there for our parent-teacher conferences."

That was the part that had made me worry, too.

"It doesn't really say in the note, but I'm thinking it must have been something she said at the conferences." I tied up the loaf of bread and put it next to the sink. "She must've been out of sorts when she went in there. You know how she talks when she's out of sorts."

I picked up the phone and listened again for a dial tone. "Nothing still." I hung up. "I need to get this thing hooked up again. If your stomach acts up at school tomorrow, they won't be able to call Valley to come get you."

"That's okay." Ruth pulled the crust off her bread and tossed it in the sink. "I'll just go lie down in the nurse's office."

I shook my head. "They won't let you do that for the whole day, Ruth. If they can't get ahold of Valley, they'll call the number on your emergency phone number card."

She started to shrug her shoulders in that so-what way she has. Until she realized what I'd been thinking.

CHAPTER TWELVE

"IF GRANDMA PAGE comes to pick me up, I'm not going with her. I'll hide in the school where no one will find me." Ruth glared at me.

"Don't you worry, Ruth," I said. "I don't think she's even allowed to leave the nursing home. And you know she's not allowed to drive a car anymore."

Ruth's arms relaxed at her sides.

"Grandma Page gets way more out of sorts than Valley does," I said. "But the thing with Grandma is, she never snaps out of it. She's out of sorts pretty much the whole day long."

"She always sounds funny when she breathes." Ruth let out a loud burst of air with a little whistle on the end.

"She can't have overnight guests where she lives

now anyway," I said. "When you go all the way to Pennsylvania, you've got to stay over," I reminded her. "They can't take care of any kids at her nursing home. They have enough to do, looking after all the old people. Besides, even if she could leave the nursing home, by the time she got all the way out here, all the doors of the school would be locked up until the next day."

"What about Aunt Dode?" Ruth licked an old patch of powdered sugar off her arm. "Is she on the emergency card?"

"I don't think so, Ruth." I wished she'd just let go of it.

"Tucker Flynn lives with his aunt. She's got a big old house with turkeys out back and a real live sheepdog that sits out front." She closed her eyes and smiled as if she was right there petting that sheepdog.

"Aunt Dode's not a real aunt," I said. "She's just Valley's sometimes-best-friend. I think you have to be a blood relative to have your name on a school emergency card. Just don't get sick until I can figure out how to get the phone back on." I started out the door. "Grab your bike. We've got some things to do." I had to make sure another note didn't come home.

"Where are we going?" Ruth walked her bike up behind me and leaned forward on her high handlebars.

"Don't you worry about a thing," I said. "I've got a whole list of ideas in my head. Just follow me."

I wished I'd thought to change my shoes like Ruth had. By the time we got downtown, my anklets had made their way deep into my patent-leather church shoes, and they were bunched up underneath my feet.

We set our bikes against the front window of the store. Ruth pointed at a *Closed* sign leaning on the inside of the glass. "The Goodwill's not even open today," she said. "We rode all the way down here for nothing."

"Not exactly." I slipped the heel of my shoe off and pulled my sock up. "We don't need to go inside."

I fixed my other sock and led her around to the side alley of the building. I nodded toward two giant wooden boxes. "All we need are the drop-off bins."

Her eyes got a wild, glazed-over look when I mentioned the drop-off bins, and I reminded myself to use different words next time.

I walked over to the bins and patted the metal dumping chute on one of them. The chute was only about half as long as my arm and plenty wide enough. "You'll fit just fine, Ruth."

She stepped back and looked as if she was getting ready to turn and head the other way, so I grabbed her by the wrist. "Calm down," I said. "I just need you to reach for a couple of things, is all." I gave her wrist a gentle squeeze. "It's a finders-keepers trip."

She squinted her eyes up at me. "This has to do with the letter, doesn't it?"

I nodded. "Partly." I looked behind me to make sure the side alley was still empty. "Valley forgot to take us school shopping this year."

Ruth shrugged.

"Well, your socks are getting loose about the tops, and your sleeves are riding way above your wrists." I tried to think back to school and Mrs. Foley. But she stared down pretty much everyone in the class, and I couldn't make myself remember if she'd done any extra looking at my clothes.

I pulled Ruth closer to the bins. "I know I could probably fit myself in the metal chute as good as you could, but there's plenty of reaching that needs to happen, and someone would have to hold my feet." I tightened my grip on her wrist. "We both know you're not strong enough for that."

She looked up in the air as if she was thinking about it.

I made my voice slow and steady, like Valley did when she was weaseling her way in or out of something. I tried to push Valley's voice out of my brain and concentrate on what I was doing. "That's why *you're* going to have to be the reacher and *I'm* going to have to be the holder."

But I kept hearing Valley's voice in my head, talking to the nurse when they were putting Ruth's cast on. "I've *told* her time and time again *not* to climb up on that dresser. And look what happened." Valley had pointed toward Ruth's new cast, but I'd been looking at Ruth's eyes. Because they knew the truth. She hadn't been anywhere near the dresser.

Ruth stayed fixed to the ground by the drop-off bin and made me wait a while before she finally answered.

"I'll be the reacher, Esther." She reared back with her free hand and karate-chopped my wrist. Hard. "Since you reached for the hamburgers. But you better not drop me."

"I *promise.*" I made a crisscross over my heart and put my hand up in front of me. "I *swear.*"

She stood stock-still in front of the chute and took two slow, deep breaths, like she always did when she was talking herself into something. She turned to me and put her hands up above her head like that Olympic gymnast, Olga Korbut. "Okay. I'm ready."

I laced my fingers together and held them down by her foot. "First, you're going to step up here. And then I'm going to get myself under you and boost you up."

She nodded and closed her eyes.

I nudged her with my shoulder. "You're going to have to open your eyes, Ruth. Or you're not going to be able to aim right with your head."

She froze her eyes like that only when she was scared, so I knew she hadn't planned on sticking her whole head in the chute. Her eyes were wide, and they were staring straight ahead.

Just when I was thinking about giving her a good elbow in the shoulder blades, she put her right foot up and stepped onto my hands.

Her arms went first. Then her whole upper body disappeared.

"You okay there, Ruth?" I was almost afraid to ask it.

Her voice sounded like she had a sweatshirt over her head. "It's dark in here and it smells like Aunt Dode."

I wrinkled up my nose. Aunt Dode smelled like back-of-the-refrigerator food.

I shifted my weight so she was almost sitting on my shoulders. "Now reach around," I said. I got a guilty heaviness in my stomach when I thought about the pink cheeseburger I'd reached for in the Dumpster. "Gather up as much as you can and I'll pull you back out."

I was surprised at how much she managed to grab. She set a big shopping bag and a small, tangled bundle on the blacktop next to us.

"Not bad, Ruth." I took the handles of the shopping bag and scooted it out of the way.

She stood back and smelled both of her arms up and down. "Hope nothing stuck on me."

I laced my fingers together again and put them out in front of her. "Come on, now. Just one more time." I nudged her legs back toward the bin. "To make sure we have enough."

One leg gave a little jerk, and I thought she might be getting ready to make a run for it, but she stepped up and went back in the chute.

"Good job, Ruth, but you don't need to kick that hard." I let her back down slowly and rubbed my arm. From the sharp quickness of it, I could tell that kick wasn't an accident.

She unwound a couple of shirts from around her wrists and set them on the blacktop.

"We'll sort through these right here." I scooped it all into one big pile and sat down on the ground. "You're going to have to stand up so I can measure on you."

The long handle of a pink pocketbook hung from her elbow, and she turned it from front to back, catching flickers of sunlight on the shiny sides.

I shook my head. "You don't need another pocketbook, Ruth. You got plenty."

But she hugged it close, and I knew there was no getting it away from her.

She grabbed a gray undershirt and held it up by the shoulder. "This is just like Mr. Lang wears when he goes out for the mail. And it would match my gray skirt."

"I think it's supposed to be white. That goes in the *no* pile." I tossed aside a couple more just like it. "They don't have any sleeves, and it's starting to get cold out." I scooped up the *no* pile and stuffed it back in the chute.

"I could use this for an Easter dress if you cut off some of the material." She wrapped a peach ruffled curtain around her middle and let it trail down her leg.

I shook my head. "It's too see-through. And Easter's not for six more months."

I pointed to the chute, but I could see her trying to stuff the curtain into her pink pocketbook. "Let me see that bag. The one with the handles." I tilted my head toward the brown shopping bag.

She pushed it in front of me with her toe.

"Shirts." They were falling out of the bag, but I noticed they had been neatly folded. I held a couple up. "They look like cowboy ones." I ran my fingers over the white buttons. "Aunt Dode has earrings made out of the same stuff as these buttons. She calls it mother-of-pearl."

Ruth pulled another shirt out of the bag and held it up to the front of her. "This would look pretty on Valley."

I nodded, but I was imagining it on me. With a real cowboy hat and some mother-of-pearl earrings.

But it was what was underneath it all that made the air around me go still. It took both of us to spread the skirt out properly. And we had to stand a solid three feet apart to get a good look.

The top looked almost like a Spanish dancer's dress. It was bright pink, and it had silver rickrack traveling down the front in zigzag paths. But the skirt was the absolutely best part. It had silver sequins sewn in small clusters all over it, and they shone like they were giving out their own light.

Ruth made the high, squeaky breath she does when she's excited. "Is there another one?"

I pushed at the empty bag with the side of my foot. "Nope." I wanted to put it on right then and there, but I knew something for sure. That dress was meant for Ruth.

"Let's get it home now, before it gets dirty." I tried to fold it back up, but her fingers held tight.

"We can't put it on you here, because it might drag on the ground." I kicked aside a cigarette butt and a bent soft-drink straw. "It could trail down and get stuck in your bike chain."

Her fingers unfolded slowly, and she adjusted the strap of the pocketbook around her neck.

I couldn't get all of the clothes to fit inside the bag again, so I ended up tying two of the cowboy shirts onto my handlebars. Then I scooched back on my banana seat so I could hold the bag in front of me.

It was slow going at first, riding with one hand. But I finally got up to a good speed, with the shirts blowing back at me along with the gold-speckled streamers on my handlebars. Ruth stood and pedaled to keep up, the shiny pink pocketbook bouncing against the front of her with each down pedal.

I thought about that note in my pouch, and my own feet pushed all the harder.

CHAPTER THIRTEEN

I UNTIED THE SHIRTS from my handlebars and set my bike down next to the hole in the front yard.

"This is taking forever, Ruth." I bent over and pushed some dirt aside with my hands. "I was digging at this for a good half an hour on Friday, and it's barely big enough to put your foot in."

Ruth wheeled her bike up beside me and took her voice down to a low whisper. "You planning on burying someone?"

"Of course not," I said. Ruth was always coming up with something to be scared about. "I'm making a rock pond." I drew an oval in the air. "I'm going to take all those rocks I painted and put them around the edge."

"Can I paint some cats on them?" Ruth was a good helper when she wanted to be.

"I'll get out the paint later." I picked up the shopping bag and turned toward the house. "We need to put this away. I'd like to do a little more digging, but we've got an evening service to go to."

The phone book was under my pillow, where I'd left it. I opened it and flipped quickly through the Yellow Pages until I got back to C. The pages were thin, and I made myself take my time tearing them out.

Ruth poked her nose over my shoulder. "Why did you tear out the dry-cleaning phone numbers?"

I shuffled the pages together and folded them carefully in half. "It's on the other side." I pointed to a sketch of a church in a bottom-corner advertisement.

Something caught the light from my window and flickered near my eye.

Ruth twirled in the middle of the carpet, the bright pink carrying the silver sequins in an orbit around her.

"It's beautiful." I sat back on my bed and followed the light path with my head. "Come here for a minute. That dress is going to fall right off you."

I was glad to see she had left her powder-blue sweatshirt on underneath it, because the dress sleeves were hanging down around her elbows.

"That would fit me perfectly." I reached out to touch the rickrack, but she got a good left claw into me. Ruth only bit the fingernails on her right hand, so her left ones were always sharp and ready to go.

"I already said it was yours." I rubbed at my arm and sat back on my bed. I would've gotten her a good one back if her insides weren't still so raw from being left.

I reached behind me for my stuffed collie and untied the long satin ribbon from its neck. "Come here." I waved her over and twirled the ribbon in the air. "The orange is a little faded, but it's plenty long enough. I play jump rope with it sometimes. Hold up your arms." I poked at her sides so she'd move her arms out of the way.

"Ouch!" She clamped her elbows into her sides.

"I need to get this around you or you'll be losing the dress before we get halfway out the door." I pried her elbows loose and looped the ribbon around her belly, crisscrossing it in the back and catching the undersides of the sleeves on the way back around the top of her chest.

She gave me a Valley look, and I got my arm away from her left side.

"It should hold like that for now, but we need to get going." I grabbed the phone-book pages from my bed. "I think we'll go with the Pentecostals next." I ran my finger down the middle column and stopped at a square advertisement with a blaze of fire in the corner. "They've got a Sunday-evening service, so we won't have to wait all the way until next week."

I undid the drawstrings on my pouch and tucked the torn-out pages inside. "The Pentecostals sound like the serious type, what with that blaze of fire and everything. They wouldn't be happy about us walking in late."

I stopped beside my dresser and carefully took my Grand Canyon plate from the wooden stand. I wiped off the layer of dust with my handkerchief and gently set it back down. Ezekiel was supposed to take us there. He'd promised. He'd shown me a picture in an old *National Geographic,* and he'd said he was going to take both me and Ruth there someday.

When I'd found the Arizona magnet, I'd known it was a sign. That's where the Grand Canyon was. The magnet had been a sign that we were going to find him soon.

I pulled my skirt down and tried to drum up what I knew about the Pentecostals. Grandma Page took me to her neighbor's church when I was back in the first grade, and I remembered those Pentecostals liked to make some noise.

When we got outside, Mr. Lang was in his driveway, hauling his garbage can out to the curb. He gave us a long wave over his head. "Hey, girls."

Mrs. Lang was behind him, carrying an extra bag of trash. "That's some dress you got on there, Ruth."

Ruth stood straight and shifted the shoulders over her sweatshirt sleeves. "We're going to the Pentecostals," she told Mrs. Lang. "They dress fancy and they don't like your knees to be showing."

I was pretty sure Ruth was mixing them up with the First Methodists, but some things were just too much trouble to explain.

Mrs. Lang handed the garbage bag to Mr. Lang. "Well, you definitely are fancy. Looks like one of the square-dancing dresses my cousin used to have."

Ruth walked ahead of me, rubbing her hip. "My bottom side's been hurting when I ride. I need for you to raise up my bike seat."

"We're walking." I headed toward the sidewalk across the street. "It'll be too dark for bikes."

"It's not dark." She squinted her eyes toward the sun.

"It will be when we're done with church," I said. "When I went with Grandma, those Pentecostals took their time getting started. The people here will probably start out with some singing and moving about." I swayed my arms from side to side above my head. "Then, after about an hour or so, the preacher will come out and yell at the crowd."

"He yells at them?" She pulled at a loose sequin.

I nodded. "You know. He points out the things you might have done wrong since last Sunday and the things you might have thought about doing wrong, and he goes on for a while. Just in case someone in the audience might have forgotten to feel sorry enough."

I could tell she had stopped paying attention to me. She was looking off to the side of my head, which was what she always did when her worrying was simmering up.

"You're not going to drop me off in the children's room, are you?" She took hold of my hand and set in with a good hard grip.

I tried to shake her loose a bit. "How many times do I have to tell you? I'm not leaving you anywhere." I looked her straight in the eye so she'd believe me. "You can't be whining at me when you get there, either. Those Pentecostals are liable to kick you right out of their evening prayer service if you make too much noise."

But right after I said it, I remembered again that the Pentecostals themselves made quite a lot of noise.

I squeezed Ruth's hand. "You're in luck today, Ruth. You don't have to worry about keeping back your hallelujahs. And you can get happy all you want. These people might even ask you back next week."

She perked right up when I said that. There was nothing Ruth liked more than a church where they did some shouting and dancing.

She swung my hand back and forth and picked up her step. "Know what, Esther?"

I did a little skip to keep up with her.

"Ezekiel's the shouting-and-dancing type of preacher." She did a quick twirl and made her dress fan out in a wide circle. "I just know it."

It actually made sense when I thought about it. Ruth loved it when people called back to the preacher, and she could get happy with the best of them. She had to have gotten it from somewhere.

I picked up the pace, and my pouch bounced against my side, reminding me about Valley. That note had to be about her. She was the only one in the family who would say something that would make a teacher stop and pay attention. I usually spent at least half of my school day trying to get Mrs. Foley not to notice me.

Then Ruth said what I'd been afraid to let myself think about. "Valley's mean streak hasn't been letting go lately, has it?" She rubbed at her elbow as if she could feel Valley right there beside her.

I shook my head slowly. "It never completely goes away now. It seems like it just slows down to a simmer and waits until the next time."

Ruth took a deep breath. "Until the next time we make her mad."

I wished we could have Ezekiel there when we gave the note to Valley. For as many times as I'd searched the years-ago section of my brain, I couldn't remember her having such a sharp edge to her when Ezekiel was around.

We were still a good block and a half away from the church when Ruth stopped short and bent down to the sidewalk, her palms flat on the cement. She tilted her head to the side slowly. "You feel that?" Her voice was just above a whisper.

The thing was, I hadn't felt a thing until the second she said it. Then the bottoms of my feet noticed the drums and the cymbals, and I did a couple of skips myself, because it was starting to seem as if it might be our lucky night.

CHaPTeR FouRTeen

"YOU SURE WE GOT the right place?" Ruth let go of my hand and stepped back from the door.

"It definitely sounds like a church." The clapping and the tambourine ringing were so loud, it looked as if Ruth's sequins were moving with the vibrations.

I pulled the phone-book page out of my pouch and checked the address with the number above the swinging door.

Amen came bursting out a couple of times between cymbal crashes. "We have definitely got the right place."

Ruth ran her fingers across the faded writing on the window next to the door.

Dinner Special— $3.99
Chicken-Fried Steak

She tilted her nose up toward the door. "I don't smell anything cooking, so it couldn't be a restaurant."

I pulled at the long handle, and the door gave way, letting out a sweaty burst of air.

"It's crowded in here." Ruth grabbed my hand again with such force I almost landed in the gray folding chair to the side of me.

"Not everyone's sitting yet," I said. "Let's find a seat up front before the music stops."

We had to twist and turn our way around the chairs, the room was so packed with people.

"It's hot." Ruth and her bony little arms were almost always cold, so that was saying a whole lot. It was as if every person in the place was breathing out and sweating on the same beat of the music.

"I want to sit up there." She pointed to the far side of the room. "You can push me around while we wait for the preacher to come out."

A line of green twisting stools was anchored to the floor in front of a narrow counter. I noticed a milkshake machine on the shelf behind the counter, its long metal spindle angled down, waiting to be mixing something up to go with that chicken-fried steak and the hallelujahs.

"Not this time, Ruth." I scanned the front of the room. "You're liable to twirl right off. Besides, you need to be paying attention."

We ended up smack-dab in the middle of the front row, which was perfect for getting an up-close look at the preacher.

"Can we sit for a while?" Ruth rubbed at the back of her ankle. "My shoes are hurting."

I shook my head. "I told you when you wanted to put your church shoes on again you'd have to double up the Band-Aids on your heels." I hooked my thumb under her elbow and pulled her up straight.

She shook my hand away. "This is like Glory Days Baptist, isn't it?"

I looked over at the choir, and it didn't seem as if they were getting ready to sit down anytime soon. "You better loosen the buckles on those shoes, because if it's like Glory Days, we'll be singing for a good forty-five minutes before we even catch sight of the preacher."

She slipped both heels out of her patent-leather shoes and stood on the backs of them.

I could see she was sinking herself into a deep sulk until the movement started to the side of her. It seemed a little early in the service for people to be getting happy, but those cymbals were crashing away.

The lady to Ruth's right had already started a hip sway, and I was afraid she was going to belt Ruth a good one, with her arms waving about like they were.

"Get over here a bit." I pulled her closer to me and watched the lady sideways out of the corner of my eye. "Stop staring, Ruth," I whispered. "It's not polite."

But then I had to stare at her full-on, too. I couldn't help myself. Because, as getting happy goes, this woman was good at it. And it seemed as if the lady next to her had gotten a lot of practice in being her assistant.

The piano music and the cymbals started to speed up, which made the woman's arm waving speed up.

The assistant knew right what to do. With a quick elbow tug she pulled that woman to the other side of her and away from Ruth. Then she leaned over toward Ruth and touched her arm. "It's okay, honey," she said. "She's got the flame in her, is all.

She's just gotten herself a good dose of the Holy Spirit."

I remembered the fire in the corner of the phone-book advertisement, and I wondered if Ezekiel had a good dose of that.

The woman was getting some fancy footwork going, and her assistant grabbed her orange straw hat and her glasses.

I noticed Ruth had stepped back into her shoes and was trying to get her feet moving like the woman's. Ruth had a steady rhythm going, and the undersides of her patent-leather toes sounded as if they had taps on them. The shiny metal kind that go *clickety-clickety* when a person knows what she's doing.

I was thinking I might like to get some good tapping in myself when I smelled that old cooked-supper smell. And it wasn't from long-ago chicken-fried steak, either. It was the smell of garlic bread and spaghetti sauce that had boiled up and burned on the bottom of the pan.

I knew Ruth had caught a whiff, too, because her body went directly from a happy sway and a tap into a shake.

Valley froze Ruth with her eyes and got in a

really good arm twist on me at the same time. It was fast and sharp and barely detectable unless you happened to be searching for it. She let go of me without any warning, and my arm hung in the air beside me, as if it had forgotten where it belonged. "Imagine my surprise," she said, "when I got home with my supplies and you were nowhere to be found."

A tiny puppy sound floated toward me, and I realized it was coming from Ruth. I took her hand and squeezed it hard to quiet her down.

"And imagine my surprise again," Valley said, "when I went outside to take some measurements and that busybody next door told me where you'd gone."

Mrs. Lang wasn't a busybody, and Valley knew it. All the anger that I thought had simmered down was back to a boil and reaching out to Ruth and me.

I could feel my hands start to shake, and the tops of my arms got all prickly, like they always did when a charged-up Valley closed in on me. I wanted to pull Ruth with me to the other side of the hip swayer, where we'd be safe.

A woman in back of us was trying to pass a

church bulletin and a hymnbook up to Valley, but Valley batted her arm away like it was a mosquito. Then, in one quick swoop, she pulled us out of that front row and on through the swinging door to the sidewalk.

CHaPteR FiFteen

VALLEY SETTLED DOWN SOME as soon as we were a few feet up that sidewalk. The sizzle seemed to have gone out of her eyes, but her feet were race-walking all the way to the pickup.

The truck was parked with one front tire on the curb and had a cockeyed tilt to it, as if it had started up a hill but changed its mind partway.

"In you go." She gave Ruth a boost and slid her over to the middle of the seat. "Go on around there, Esther."

I knew to be quick about it. Once Valley had her mind wrapped around something, she didn't like to wait for others.

I barely had my other leg on the seat when the truck lurched forward and bumped off the curb.

Johnny Cash sang at me from the eight-track cassette in the dashboard about a train coming, and I was thinking he had no idea. And neither did the cars around us. When Valley had a notion, she drove that pickup like a big old freight train, blasting in and out between the cars and barely missing the ones that thought they were safely parked. There were streaks along the bottoms of the doors on the pickup where she had caught a door handle or two.

I saw a cemetery coming up and elbowed Ruth to remind her. She gulped a quick gasp of air and held her breath. I was already holding mine, on account of Valley's driving. We passed the last gravestone, and I tapped Ruth's knee sharply so she wouldn't turn blue.

"I told you girls to stop looking for him. It's a big waste of your time." She turned Johnny Cash down a little and turned her voice up. "I just wanted to make the house nice for all of us. When I got home, you were nowhere to be found."

Valley stepped on the gas, and I hooked my arm through Ruth's.

"I want to get everything I need for the redecorating before I start." Valley leaned into her steering wheel. "I don't want to have to stop midway to go get something." The truck made a half-circle skid, and I ended up pressed against Ruth, who was squashed sideways against Valley, when we came to a stop.

Valley was halfway out the door by the time she turned the engine off, and I had to give one long scoot across the seat to catch up.

I nudged Ruth. "Hurry up now. She's practically across the parking lot already."

"I thought the bowling alley was closed." Ruth followed me toward the giant wooden bowling pin in the far corner of the parking lot.

The painted-on letters used to say RIVERSIDE LANES, but most of the *R* was worn away, and the last half of the *Lanes* part was broken clean off. I couldn't figure out what the bowling alley had to do with Valley's redecorating.

"I thought so, too." I looked behind me at all the cars in the parking lot. The lines for the parking spaces had long since faded away, and people had pulled in every which way, making it look like a page from my book of pencil mazes.

Ruth pointed at the faded ball and pins on the double doors. "I've never known Valley to do any bowling."

"Valley does whatever comes to mind for her." I put all my weight against the door on the right and pushed in. It gave way with a cracking sound, as if the foggy glass wasn't quite solid in the frame anymore.

A long counter stretched out to the left of us, with shelves of dusty brown-and-red bowling shoes lined up in neat rows behind it.

"You suppose Valley already got us some shoes?" I raised my voice and leaned down so Ruth could hear me over all the noise.

But the sound wasn't the crash of balls on the bowling pins. It was just plain loud voices of people. And when we made our way around the corner of the counter, I could see there were plenty of them.

Tables were set up in long rows, sideways, over the gutters. Every possible space was taken up. People had even put up their tables and chairs where the pins used to set down.

"A flea market!" Ruth bounced on her toes and spun her sequined dress around in a fluttery circle. There was nothing Ruth and I liked more than a yard sale, and a flea market was like dozens of good yard sales tied together.

"It's a big one, all right." I wound my way slowly between the tables, towing Ruth and her sequins along behind me. I wrapped the tail end of her ribbon belt around my wrist and got a good hard grip on her hand. Valley was on a finders-keepers trip, and we needed to keep up.

The area above the bowling lanes looked like the parking lot outside. People had angled their card tables anywhere they could get them.

I squeezed Ruth's hand. "You spot a sign of Valley anywhere?"

She shook her head quickly, but I could tell she hadn't even been trying to find her. She was too busy scanning the tables to see what all the people were selling. Some of it was like what we'd put back in the bins at the Goodwill: things with their working parts missing or splintered, bits and pieces hardly worth keeping.

Ruth made her way to the edge of the table closest to us. "Oh . . ." Her voice got heavy and hoarse, as if she was sad and scared at the same time. "They're sick. All of them. . . ."

She was right. I knew it as soon as I saw them. Scattered parts of used-to-be dolls. Heads and bodies, without an arm or two. Some were still dressed, but others had the naked arms bent up next to the bodies but not connected. And the far end of the table was the saddest part: rows and rows of arms and legs, with nothing to attach themselves to.

It was the loneliest thing I'd ever seen. I never

used just one of anything in my garden. If you used at least two of everything, something always belonged to something else.

"Come on, Ruth." I gave her ribbon belt a quick tug. "We've got to find Valley."

She turned away and shrugged off my hand, because we both knew there was just too much else to look at.

Some of the tables were piled with possibilities. And those were the tables that were hard to get to. You had to stand back to catch a peek, because there were so many people crowded around, sifting through the stacks.

I thought I caught a glimpse of an aqua-blue sleeve at a table a couple of lanes away, but when I looked hard, my eyes couldn't sift through the flock of people.

I figured Ruth had seen it, too, when I saw a flash of sequins. Ruth ducked around some legs and grabbed hands, getting herself right up close to the table in front of us. I clamped another good hold on her ribbon belt, and she hauled me with her to a corner of the table. I could see right away it wasn't Valley she was scrambling for.

"Oh . . ." Ruth's voice was half breath, half squeak. "It's perfect."

The house part was made of tin, with three square rooms in a row, and all the tiny rugs and windows were painted on.

"Look at the chairs!" Ruth bent in close to the room in the middle. It had a wobbly table that looked as if one leg had somehow caught fire and melted down a half inch or so. The tiny white plastic chairs were just like the ones in our kitchen at home.

She moved her hand toward the blue plastic couch in the living room and was just about to close her hand around it when a long flowered sheet came billowing down over her arm to cover the table.

A voice crackled from loudspeakers in the ceiling. "Ten minutes until closing. Vendors, please secure your wares. Customers, please complete your purchases."

"Let's go, Ruth!" I pulled her away from the table by her elbow and tried to search out Valley across the way.

I looked for a streak of aqua blue as people moved toward the doors. It was hard to get even a glimpse of Valley, with all the movement going on around us. Sellers slid their goods into big boxes, and some just covered up their tables with sheets or blankets, keeping them ready and waiting for the next day.

We made our way diagonally to the back of the bowling alley, climbing over the lanes and weaving through the long tables. I pointed to the next lane. "I thought I saw her over there."

But when we hopped over the ball return, all we found was an old woman slowly pushing her way back down the lane, trying to keep her walker out of the gutter. And as the crowd thinned to almost no one, I knew something for dead sure without Ruth even saying it.

Ruth took a deep breath and looked sideways at me. "No Valley."

CHapTer SixTeen

"SHE'S DONE A RUNNER, hasn't she?" I thought about checking the bathrooms just to be sure, but I knew how Valley felt about public restrooms. She said they were havens for disease and she'd just as soon use the bushes outside.

Ruth raised her skirt out wide and sank to the edge of the gutter. She got that closed-up look about the face that made it really hard to talk to her. "We never even got to see the preacher."

She was right. Ezekiel could've been right under our noses and we'd missed him. I shouldn't have been paying so much attention to the woman next to us when we were at the Pentecostal church. Maybe then I could've caught a glimpse of Ezekiel.

I looked out at the almost empty parking lot. "It's pretty dark out there."

Ruth turned toward the parking lot and squinted up her eyes. "Are you sure she's not in the truck waiting for us to come out?"

I shook my head. Valley never waited around for anyone. "We could maybe sleep here tonight. It's way too far to walk home. Especially in the dark."

But I knew even before the words were out of my mouth I couldn't do that to Ruth. And when someone switched off most of the lights near us, I was sorry I'd had the thought.

I followed her eyes toward the table with the doll parts. A stray arm poked out from beneath the sheet cover. I could hear Ruth's breath catch in a sharp burst toward the back of her throat, and I was thinking it sounded like the beginning of one of her screams.

I pushed her toward the front door while she was still building energy, and we were a good twenty to twenty-five running steps across the parking lot when she got herself properly worked up.

The scream didn't sound half as bad when it happened outside. I looked around the parking lot and tried to act as if nothing was wrong, in case someone happened to be paying attention. But no one so much as looked in our direction. A woman under the streetlight across the parking lot was loading a couple of cardboard boxes into the trunk of her car. She didn't even glance over her shoulder at us.

I tried not to peek at Ruth myself. Paying attention to her could give her new momentum.

I tossed a tiny piece of broken asphalt in front of me and played a fake game of hopscotch to wait her out.

Sure enough, before I was done with my game, the screams had softened into screechy bursts of air. She had finally quieted herself into a squeaky machine part.

I kicked aside a chunk of asphalt. "You finished?"

She sank to the ground, her skirt poufing out like a parachute around her.

I saw the tiny piece of blue plastic fall to the ground beside her. "Oh, Ruth. Not again."

She turned, trying to hide the little couch with her leg.

"Why couldn't you have just let it be?" I thought about the little tin living room with the now bare painted-on rug. "They'll notice the missing davenport right away."

"I was just borrowing it for a bit." She scooped

it up and cupped it in her hand, and I knew she hadn't once thought about giving it back. It wasn't a borrow. *Charlotte's Web* flashed to the front of my brain. It was a flat-out swipe.

I put my hand out to her. "Let's get going. It's a long walk, and we've got school tomorrow."

She stood up slowly, holding her hand to her back like an old woman.

We had barely made our way out of the parking lot when I knew we couldn't walk the whole way home. Ruth was moving as if she was ice-skating. She had slipped her heels out, and she was walking on the backs of her church shoes, pushing them forward on the pavement with every jerky step.

We passed the movie theater, and I wished I'd thought to bring some money. It would've been a perfect place to wait out the dark.

But as I steered Ruth around a woman's laundry basket at the bus stop, I realized we might not have to walk the rest of the way home.

We turned the corner and pushed open the door to the left of Leona's Sit and Spin. We stood at the bottom of a steep, narrow staircase. The machines were clanking and humming on the other side of the wall.

"You be real quiet now." I looked back at Ruth. "Aunt Dode is most likely working." One of her Spanish records was on, so I knew she had a customer.

I pointed at Ruth's feet. "Put your heels back in. Aunt Dode won't like you clomping up the stairs. She'll make us turn back around and go home, dark or not."

She put her finger to the back of her right ankle and shoehorned her heel back in. But just one foot. That was Ruth for you. She didn't like to listen the whole way. She raised her right foot and put it softly on the step behind me, dragging her left shoe behind her with a clomp.

The door at the top of the stairs opened into Aunt Dode's kitchen. We went in. Aunt Dode jumped up and rushed toward us. At first I thought she was happy to see us. Then I saw that her face didn't have one trace of happy on it.

"Oh, no!" She put her arms around our shoulders and guided us back to the top of the stairs. "You can go right back the way you come!" She stood on her tiptoes so she could see over Ruth and me. "Where is she?" Her eyes darted from side to side and down to the bottom of the staircase.

"Where's who?" Ruth made like she was going

to move forward into the kitchen, but Aunt Dode stood firm, blocking the way.

"Valley Page is not setting foot in my house ever again!" An angry burst of spit came toward me when Aunt Dode said Valley's name.

"But it's just us." Ruth stepped to the side so Aunt Dode could see the empty steps. "It's me and Esther."

I thought enough time had gone by. I figured she had stopped being mad at Valley. But her foot was planted on the floor in front of us like a heavy rock.

"Looks like you found a nice place." I tried to make my voice sound friendly, as if we were pleasant, interesting company that you'd love to have sipping a little lemonade in your living room.

I took in a quick sniff. "And it doesn't even have the burnt barbecue smell like the old place."

Then I realized that mentioning the fire was the one thing I probably shouldn't have done, because Aunt Dode went to shut the door.

But then Ruth leaned her head back and lined up her eyes with Aunt Dode's. "We got left." She said it in a soft voice, and Aunt Dode had to lean forward to listen. "Valley did a runner."

I moved in close to Ruth. "It's too dark to walk home."

Aunt Dode took a deep breath and slowly stepped to the side. "Come in, then." She shook her head and mumbled something I couldn't quite make out. "But you need to go right to the living room. I've got a customer." She glanced over her shoulder and switched into her fortune-telling voice. "She's in the bathroom, but she'll be right out."

Her customer had a rain hat covering her head, even though there wasn't a speck of bad weather outside. It was the plastic kind that Valley always kept in her purse. The kind that folded up like an accordion, and when you took your time with it, it could actually fit in the palm of your hand. The woman sat in the chair across from Aunt Dode. She hunched over the table on her elbows, her plastic-covered head in her hands.

Aunt Dode sat on the edge of her chair and held a pair of men's eyeglasses in front of her chest, making the painted-on wolf on her big T-shirt appear as if it were looking through one of the lenses at us. She spoke to the woman with an accent, which I'd seen her do with her out-of-town customers. "I can feel your husband is near." She held the glasses in front of her lightbulb-shaped nose and closed her eyes. "He will return to you within the week."

I grabbed Ruth around the wrist and pressed my

side along the kitchen counter, trying to make myself blend in with the seafoam-green cabinets.

Aunt Dode pushed her chair back loudly, and I froze for a second, willing Ruth with my mind to stay quiet.

But Aunt Dode wasn't coming after us. She was readjusting herself in her chair, leaning in toward the woman and pressing the eyeglasses to her forehead. She had on what Valley called her fortune-telling face—sort of a mixture between a frown and looking like she had to go to the bathroom real bad. One side of the glasses got tangled in Dode's thin black hair, and she pulled her hair back with her thumbs so it hung over her shoulders. She pressed herself against her chair and shuffled her wide white sneakers on the linoleum. Her long cornflower-blue cotton skirt rode up, and I could see the blotchy red skin above the fold of one of her anklets.

Ruth reached for a bag of Wonder bread on the counter and tucked it under her arm.

Aunt Dode turned her head ever so slightly toward us, and I galloped out the other door into the living room, towing Ruth behind me by the ribbon belt.

Ruth sank down in the pillow corner beside the purple lava lamp. She pulled out a slice of Wonder bread and folded it in half on her lap. "Want one?" She squished it together in her palms, making a doughy white lump.

I shrugged and held out my hand. It had been a while since my olive-and-margarine sandwich.

"Don't get any crumbs around." I took my pouch off and set it beside me on the sofa. That note inside was only made of paper, but in my mind it was weighing down my little purse like a slug of lead.

CHAPTER SEVENTEEN

MY SKIN WAS SWEATY as I peeled the side of my face from the plastic on the couch. Aunt Dode kept her apartment like the Florida Everglades.

Ruth was still asleep on the pillows beneath the lava lamp. Her dress spilled out around her, making a sparkly sequined blanket. She had the bag of Wonder bread tucked under her arm.

I nudged her knee gently with my toe. "Come on, there, Ruth. We've got to get started for school."

She pushed herself up on one elbow and flopped back down. "Can't you write me a note like last week? I'm tired."

I shook my head and pulled on her skirt. "That's too many notes. They start to make phone calls and ask questions when you've got too many notes."

I picked up my pouch and looped it over one shoulder.

I already had enough notes to worry about. And now the weekend was over and Mrs. Foley was going to be expecting an answer to hers. I swallowed over the dry patch in my throat and tried to come up with what I could say.

"How about we just go in late, then?" Ruth sat up and smoothed her skirt across her lap. "An hour or two." She looked toward the kitchen door. "Maybe Aunt Dode will make us pancakes."

Even Aunt Dode got a good laugh going at that one. She walked into the living room with a Styrofoam cup of coffee and motioned me over on the couch. "Pancakes, huh?" She wrinkled up her nose like she was considering it. "Just how does one go about making pancakes?"

Ruth leaned in as if she was getting ready to tell her.

Aunt Dode held the cup up to her mouth and took a loud sip of her coffee. "Order 'em off a menu. That's the way to do it." She held out a dusty glass candy dish from the coffee table. "Breakfast is served."

"No, thank you." I waved it away, because that same dish of hard candy had been on the coffee table at her old place. That Christmas ribbon candy was wavy and pretty, but it stuck together in one clump and would probably chisel a corner of your jaw right off if you bit into it.

As if she had read my mind, Aunt Dode tried to give it a nudge in the dish. But it held fast to the center. She set it back down. "If I give this away to you, I won't have any refreshments left to give my customers."

Ruth moved her hand forward on her lap, as if she might still be thinking about breaking off a piece.

"Where's your mother?" Aunt Dode had her half-listening look about the eyes. The one she saved up for kids and for Valley when she was out of sorts.

Ruth talked around a mouthful of Wonder bread. "She did a runner."

Aunt Dode finally gave us her eyes straight on. "She dropped you off here? I can't be taking care of you two. I've got to work." She shook her head. "It's not the type of job where you can have kids around. I need to concentrate, and so do my customers."

She put her pinky finger in her coffee and stirred it around. "Your mother just goes full speed ahead without thinking things through. And when she's in her blue moods, she doesn't do much thinking of any kind."

She slurped some coffee from the end of her pinky. "Like when she fell asleep with those cigarettes of hers. I'd told her a million times to put those out when she got sleepy." She sucked in her cheeks. "I lost about everything I owned in that fire, and she herself was lucky to have gotten out of there alive."

I had been with Ruth on a finders-keepers trip when the fire happened. I'd thought it was the noontime siren at the fire station at first, until those sirens had kept going.

Aunt Dode nodded at Ruth. "I never minded watching you girls every once in a while. You two never gave me any trouble. But I can't have Valley around here anymore. I lost a lot of my regular customers after the fire. They felt that me and my place were bad luck."

Ruth did a quick crisscross over her heart, like she always did when anyone mentioned bad luck.

"Now I've got a chance here for a fresh start." Aunt Dode let out a quick laugh. "I have declared myself Valley-free."

I wasn't sure what to say to that. I wasn't sure how I'd feel if I had to be Valley-free.

"I thought she was just plain fun and good times all those years ago, when we worked together at the Mark and Pack." Valley had a half smile on her face, as if she was remembering something in the far-back part of her brain. "And she was the best assistant I had when she used to help me out with my business." Her smile disappeared real suddenly. "But she could be the worst, too." She narrowed her eyes at me. "She taking her pills at all?"

I shrugged. "Not for a while, I don't think. Except for the yellow ones. The ones that she takes when her body needs to sleep but her mind won't let her."

Aunt Dode licked the end of a tissue and wiped at yesterday's makeup under her eyes. "Soon as she feels better, she stops taking her pills. Thinks she doesn't need them."

"You find that lady's lost husband?" Ruth looked toward the door as if Aunt Dode had conjured up the missing husband in the kitchen. "From last night?"

I ignored Ruth and leaned in close to Aunt Dode. "Maybe you could help us find Ezekiel."

"I'm too tired for this." She sipped at her coffee and shook her head. "Each time you ask, you hear the same answer from me, so you need to stop asking and face the facts."

I tapped the side of her cup. "So maybe, after you've finished your coffee, you could get out your fortune-telling stuff and help us find him. Once you get warmed up, it shouldn't take long."

Aunt Dode had a thicker stubborn steak than Valley. She set her cup down next to the candy dish and moved in so our foreheads were almost touching. "Leonard's not coming back, Esther. You need to get that in your head. And you need to have a long talk with your mother." She wiped at a dribble of coffee on her chin with her makeup tissue.

"Why are you always calling him Leonard?" Ruth wrinkled her nose.

"It's his given name." Aunt Dode sighed. "I don't believe in nicknames. Especially when the person's long gone."

I hated it when people gave up on Ezekiel like that, especially Aunt Dode. I wasn't going to give up, because I could see in her eyes that she wanted to help me and Ruth.

"I tried to call your mother to come get you last night." She nodded at the phone on the end table. "But the number was disconnected."

"Valley bought a necklace with the phone money." Ruth made like she was putting one on herself. "It was a must-have for the fall."

Aunt Dode rolled her eyes. "And my car is on the fritz, so I can't exactly drive you home myself." She stood up. "I can't have Valley in my house anymore. I've learned my lesson with her. Since Leonard's been gone, trouble just seems to follow her. Nothing against you two, but she's going to have to find someone else to watch her kids."

Aunt Dode let out a long puff of air and handed me two crumpled dollar bills from the pocket of her bathrobe. "Buy yourselves some cups of coffee downstairs and get to school. What time's it start? Nine? Ten?" You could tell she'd never had any kids, because she never knew a whole lot about things like that.

"Thanks, Aunt Dode." I combed my fingers through my hair and stood up. "Let's go, Ruth." I looked out the window at the pink sky and checked the clock next to the lava lamp. "We only have a couple of hours, and we've still got to stop by home and brush our teeth."

Ruth stood up and smoothed out her skirt. She was staring at those sequins with a dreamy smile on her face, and I knew that she was going to give me a hard time about changing her clothes.

We made our way down the stairs and out through the Laundromat.

"Pick up your feet, Ruth. You're not going to school with all that Wonder bread stuck in your teeth, and I'm not getting another tardy slip."

She stopped and squinted up at Aunt Dode's window. "How come Aunt Dode always calls Ezekiel 'Leonard'?"

I pushed at her side with my elbow. "You heard what she said. She said it's his nickname. Valley's always called him Ezekiel. Maybe it's his middle name or something."

She held out the bag of Wonder bread with both hands and kicked it up in front of her with each step on the sidewalk. Nothing slowed Ruth down more than someone trying to nudge her along.

I was hungry for something besides Ruth's squashed bread, and each kick of that bag was cranking up my annoyance with her. I knew the mean was creeping into my head, but I couldn't help myself.

So I went ahead.

Way far ahead.

Like I was leaving her. I could almost feel her

scream getting ready behind me, but I couldn't make my feet stop.

I could hear the clicks of her church shoes, closer and closer together, as she tried to catch up. But that cranky mad I was feeling just made me speed up.

The clicks were about catching up with me when I heard squeaky brakes pull up beside me.

I heard John Denver singing about the Rocky Mountains, and Valley leaned out the driver's-side window of the pickup. "I came back to the bowling alley, but you girls were already gone." Her words spilled from her mouth as if she couldn't get them out fast enough, and her eyes had the wide-open look they got when she had forgotten to go to bed.

"It was dark, Valley. You know how Ruth is afraid of the dark." Even though I was a few inches away from her, I could tell she wasn't really listening. Her mind was most likely already speeding past us. I wanted to turn around and get Ruth out of there, because we didn't even need Valley right then. We had needed her last night.

"I ran into a woman who had a brand-new living-room couch for sale. It would have matched that shag carpeting I put in." She closed her eyes as if she was picturing it in her mind. "But I got it all the way in our living room, and the color was all wrong. So I had no choice but to rip off the old upholstery fabric."

She kept going on and on about that couch, and all I wanted her to do was go on home. I hated the way Ruth stood there, her knees all stiff, holding tight to that bag of Wonder bread.

Valley didn't say it, so I did. I got as close as Ruth would let me. "You okay, Ruth?"

She wouldn't answer me. She dug her clicky heels into the sidewalk and stared straight ahead. If I'd known Valley was going to show up like that, I wouldn't have been so mean. I'd have waited for Ruth to catch up.

I whispered down near Ruth's ear. "Good news is, I think she's let go of the old notion. We can probably stop hiding all of our electric stuff."

She gave a little sniff and moved a tiny bit closer to me, so I knew she was listening.

Valley stared down at us from the window of her pickup as if she'd just remembered we were there. She pointed at both of us and to the seat next to her. "Let's go. You girls have school now, don't you?"

Ruth went around to the other side of the truck, but I hung back for a second. It sounded as if John

Denver's voice had gotten a little louder, like he might be trying to warn me as I climbed in after her and pulled the door shut.

Valley put the truck in gear and pulled away from the curb. Even though her words were spilling out a million miles an hour, she was driving the truck so slowly I was thinking Ruth and I could've kept up with her on our bikes.

I tried to keep my eyes facing forward, too, because I didn't like the nasty stares the people in the other cars were giving us when they had to drive around. I knew their minds were set on getting to work, and Valley was right in the middle of both lanes of the road, not even trying to scoot over. She never noticed when she was in the way. When she was out of sorts, she didn't tend to see things to the left or right of her. Especially people.

I reached out for Ruth and held her tight to my side, because the school was coming up and I saw which direction we were headed.

Over the curb in the back of the school.

Valley drove right over the sidewalk and onto the playground through the gap where the cyclone fence was broken. She coasted to a slow stop without turning off the engine. If I'd rolled down the window on my side, I could've reached out and touched a rusty orange bar of the jungle gym.

"C'mon, Ruth." I grabbed her hand. "The bell's going to ring."

She looked out at the sky just starting to brighten over the slide, and she turned to me with her mouth partway open, because she knew as well as I did that bell wasn't going to ring anytime soon.

But then she glanced back at Valley and those wide eyes of hers, and she followed me out of the truck.

CHapter Eighteen

I WATCHED THE WHEELS of Valley's pickup roll out the way they'd come in, and I rested against the bottom bar of the jungle gym. The backs of my legs were cold, and I wished I'd thought to put on tights before we went to the Pentecostals' last night. I didn't let my breathing slow down until I knew that pickup was for sure carrying Valley away from us.

Ruth climbed halfway up and stopped, her white patent-leather heels pointing down at me. "I forgot the Wonder bread in the truck."

I brushed the fronts of my teeth with the side of my finger, but it didn't do much good. My mouth tasted like I'd licked some rust off the jungle gym. "We've got plenty of time." I felt for the crumpled dollar bills in my pouch. "We'll go get something to eat."

Home wasn't a good idea right then, with Valley out of sorts like she was. It was best to wait her out somewhere else.

Ruth climbed down and sat next to me, kicking up the sawdust shavings on the ground. "What's that you've got in your hand?"

I held the piece of paper out to her. "It's a list I was working on at Aunt Dode's. A kind of check-list, so we remember important things."

I tapped the list. "You need to help me remember to look at this every morning. Especially on school days."

She read the first one slowly. "'Check neck and fingernails.'"

I nodded. "People are always saying to wash behind your ears. But it's your neck you really need to be worrying about." I stretched out my neck and turned my head from side to side. "Especially the front of it. That's the part people see when you're standing in front of them."

Ruth rubbed her hand along her neck below her chin and checked her fingers for any dirt. "I'm good." She moved in close to me. "So are you." She held up the paper.

"The next one says to check socks for holes and check dress hems when you are sitting down." I stopped and raised my foot in the air. "Only worry about the holes that you can see. For example, I've got a couple of holes in my sock right now, but they're around the toe area, so I'm not going to count that."

"What else?" Ruth bent over to get a good look at her socks.

"That's as far as I've got." I put it in my pouch with the note. "We can add more to it later. The whole point is not to give people something to be nosy about."

Ruth stood up. "Let's get us some doughnuts." She raised one eyebrow like she did when she had a good idea. "*Day-old* doughnuts!"

It was great thinking, I had to hand it to her. Day-old meant you could get three times as many for your money.

We made our way to the street on the other side of the school. I sniffed out those doughnuts from the Goodwill parking lot around the corner. The smell of sugar and fried dough along the whole block was always so powerful that even the clothes you bought from inside the Goodwill had a doughnut smell to them.

The DOUGHNUT HOUSE sign used to look so fancy. It was lit up red like Christmas all year round. But the *Dough* part had blinked out at least a year ago, and now the red *nut House* sign flashed on and off like one of Valley's notions.

I stopped by the front door. "Hold on a second, Ruth." I grabbed her shoulder for balance and shook the sawdust shavings out of one of my shoes. "I really need to take my socks off. I can feel wood pieces between my toes."

But I knew Ruth was hungry for those doughnuts, and she moved to the side real fast, making me roll my ankle.

"A little fancy just for school, don't you think?" Gull Garvin was coming out of the door with a white paper bag, licking at the corner of a maple bar.

She looked my church clothes up and down and wiped her knuckle at some pale brown frosting in the corner of her mouth.

Ruth's eyes rested on Gull's dark green corduroys. "You're going to get sent home."

Gull tore her maple bar in two and handed us each a big piece.

"Oh, I don't want to take your breakfast." The smell of that sweet maple frosting was making my stomach growl.

Gull opened the bag and tipped it to the side. "I got plenty. Day-old comes six to a bag. I'll get sick if I eat the whole thing."

Ruth held her half under her nose and breathed in deep before she took a bite. "This isn't Friday. No girls wearing pants to school except on Fridays." She chewed around her words with her know-it-all voice, which I thought was pretty nervy, seeing as she was eating up Gull's doughnut.

Gull reached into her bag and bit into another maple bar. "I won't get sent home."

I knew she was right. The principal had given up after the first couple of weeks of school this year. He'd call Mrs. Garvin up and tell her about the rule, but Gull's mom had too many kids to worry about a rule like that. And Gull would come back to school the next day wearing pants.

I pulled the two dollars out of my pouch and held them out. "I'll get us something to drink."

Gull waved them away with her hand and grabbed a tall bottle of chocolate Yoo-hoo out of her coat pocket. "We can share."

I leaned over to Gull when Ruth wasn't looking. "Have her drink last." I tilted my head in Ruth's direction. "She spits back in when she's drinking."

Gull nodded. "My brother Wayne does that."

I shook my head. "The one that smokes?"

Gull unscrewed the lid and took a long swig. Then she held the bottle out to me. "That's what makes it extra bad when he does it."

She rolled down the top of the waxy white bag. "I might have the last two for lunch. If you sit with me, I'll give you some."

Ruth reached for the Yoo-hoo. "We get free lunch." She licked at a dribble on the outside of the bottle. "You don't need a ticket or anything. The cooks know your name, and they let you take a tray without paying."

I'd been trying to tell her that free lunch wasn't something you go around mentioning, but Gull didn't seem to mind one bit.

"We got free lunch for a while at my old school, after my mom had the last baby." Gull must've forgotten what I said about Ruth spitting back in, because she took another long drink.

"My mom couldn't be doing her Avon orders with the new baby, and my dad was only working part-time, so we were a little short on cash. I think they automatically give you free lunch after number eight." She tossed the empty bottle in a trash can in the corner of the parking lot. "I don't remember Mama saying anything. I just remember the cook telling me to pick up a tray from the stack and slide it through the line."

Gull stared at the side of my head and smoothed her hand over a piece of my hair. "You sleep funny last night?" She reached into the front pocket of her striped T-shirt and held out a black plastic comb.

"Maybe a little." I pulled the comb through my hair. Aunt Dode's fortune-telling voice always gave me strange dreams. It made my thoughts spin around and got me wondering too much when I should've been relaxing.

"You coming back to First Methodist tonight?" She lifted up her pant leg and pulled a church bulletin out of her tube sock.

I tugged the comb through a tangle. "Tonight?"

"It's family Bible study, which means really good snacks. Brownies, pie, Goofy Grape Kool-Aid. . . ." She opened the bulletin and pointed to the second page. " 'This Week at First Methodist Church.' I'll write down the time for you, but I can't give this away. My mom saves them every week. She's got a whole box of these in the living room. Just in case she has to look back at a Bible verse or who was in need of prayer a few weeks ago." She folded it up and shoved it in her sock. "My mom saves just about everything."

"We can't go tonight." I had to make sure Ruth didn't get in the pickup with Valley. We needed to stay put, safe at home. There was something in Valley's voice this morning that made the arm-twist spot by my elbow give off a steady pulsing ache, as if it was expecting something.

"I'll save you a seat, just in case." Gull never liked to take no for an answer.

But I knew we wouldn't be going to First Methodist tonight. Valley had left Ruth twice in the last few days. She would never have done that when Ezekiel was around. He had a quiet, reminding way about him that made people be on their best behavior. He didn't need a list, because he automatically remembered the really important things. We had to find him.

And I was getting another idea.

CHAPTER nineteen

I PUSHED MY CHAIR BACK and rooted around inside my desk for a clean tissue. The paper bag was where it was every morning, in the front left corner. Mrs. Foley had never said a word, but I knew she was the one who left the sandwich bags in my desk. I started finding them around the third week of school. The napkin inside the bag smelled just like her. Like the cinnamon-and-sugar toast Ruth and I had when we snuck into vacation Bible school last summer. I unfolded the top of the bag and gave it a quick sniff. Roast beef. It was almost always roast beef on Monday. Too bad it wasn't Friday, because the last two Fridays there had been a chocolate-chip cookie to go with it.

I fished a tissue out of the back of my desk and

shook some pencil shavings from it. Twisting up a corner, I gave it a good lick. Then I wiped at the long reddish brown streak on the bottom hem of my dress. It looked like part jungle-gym rust and part maple bar, and I could see it wasn't coming off anytime soon.

Mrs. Foley walked to the big green paper cutter on the side counter by the sink. She had on those spongy, quiet teacher shoes that could sneak up on you without any warning. "Five more minutes to review your words from last week," she said, "and we'll be starting the spelling test."

She sliced a thin stack of lined paper into two narrow strips. Then she walked between the rows, passing them out. "Please put the proper heading at the top, and don't forget to number down the left side."

I looked down at my list of words and wished I'd remembered to study over the weekend.

Mrs. Foley stopped next to me, and I was afraid she was going to ask me to spell a few words.

"Say, Esther?" She bent over my desk, so I couldn't pretend I hadn't heard her. "Did your mother send a response to the note I gave you to take home?"

I sniffed a little and blew my nose on the tissue

to buy myself some time. "My mom's been working graveyard shift, so my aunt Dode's been watching us. I tried to give it to Aunt Dode, but it had Valley's name on it, and she didn't want to open someone else's mail."

Mrs. Foley lowered her voice to just above a whisper. "I tried to call your mother on Friday evening, and I just got a recording that said your phone number was out of service." She squatted down beside me. "Is everything all right?"

I thought fast and came up with a good lie that was so smooth I halfway believed it myself. "The bill got knocked off the counter and got stuck behind the stove, so Valley forgot to pay it. It should be working again in the next week or two."

"Oh well." Mrs. Foley stood back up. "These things happen. Please tell her to get in touch as soon as possible."

I made myself push Valley out of my mind, and I tried to concentrate on my spelling test. Gull sat across the aisle and one row up from me. She must have known I didn't study, because every time she finished writing a word she'd slide her paper to the corner of her desk and angle it toward me.

But I didn't even let myself glance in her direction,

because there was no way I was going to cheat on my spelling test. Those roast-beef sandwiches would never taste the same if I did.

Even if I hadn't studied, it was good to be at school. I didn't have to think about Valley or Ezekiel or even Ruth. And if I'd been able to push aside the nagging worry of what the note was about, it would have been an almost perfect day.

In the last hour, Mrs. Foley put out all kinds of art supplies so we could start our relief maps of the United States. Most of the kids were just slapping their clay on their piece of cardboard any old way, but I took my time with mine. I sketched out the way I wanted it to look, just like I do when I'm making a new garden. It was all in the planning.

Then, because my area was the neatest and most organized, Mrs. Foley let me take home a whole shoebox full of extra supplies. She said she was cleaning out all the old stuff from the shelves of her art closet. I wished I could get a look inside that closet, because when I lifted up the lid of the shoe-box, I noticed a package of brand-new marking pens inside.

I met Ruth by the jungle gym. She was swoosh-ing her skirt back and forth in front of her, making the sequins catch the sun. "Let's go back to the Goodwill." She twirled in a quick circle. "I want to find me another one of these dresses."

I grabbed her hand and tried to hurry her up a little. "Not right now. We've got to go home."

I knew I was going to have to get that dress off her, too. The sequins on that thing were like a lit-up sign telling her teacher to send home a note. It'd be even worse if she tried to wear it to school tomorrow, because it would have another day's worth of Ruth-type dirt and grime for them to write about.

I pulled her to me. "I've got a good idea, and you're going to need to help me with it."

She must've liked the sound of that, because she sped her church shoes right along and didn't even whine about taking a rest break the whole way home.

As we turned the corner for our house, I could see Valley's truck parked cockeyed up on the grass. She had stopped just short of the hole I'd been digging.

I gave Ruth's hand a squeeze. "She's home." My heart switched over to the quick speeding-up kind of beats that it saved for Valley.

Ruth ran across the driveway and over the grass to the house. She stood on tiptoe and pressed her nose flat against the dining-room window. "I don't see her."

The kitchen door was unlocked, but Valley wasn't anywhere to be found. If she had gone somewhere without the car, she couldn't be far. And that meant Ruth and I didn't have a whole lot of time.

I held the brown lunch bag out to Ruth.

"Is it roast beef?" She pulled the waxed paper to the side and took a long sniff.

I nodded. "It's Monday." I had wanted to eat the whole thing along with my school lunch. They only give you about a quarter cup of noodles on spaghetti day. "Don't forget to save me half," I said. "Just take a bite or two while I look for Valley."

The house was so quiet, she couldn't be inside. But when I got to the living room, I knew without a doubt that she'd been there. One of the side walls was almost completely knocked out. Clumps of plaster and wide pieces of wall were all over the floor. In one spot you could see through to the bathroom.

Ruth stood back a few feet, forgetting to chew her bite of roast-beef sandwich. "Looks like Valley's redecorating the whole house."

I hoped and prayed she hadn't touched our room, but I knew, without even taking one step inside, she'd been hard at work in there, too.

Our door was off its hinges and leaning against the wall in the hallway. I felt a breeze coming at me from beside Ruth's bed. It hadn't been even a touch of cold outside, but that bit of air made my forehead freeze up and get all tingly, like it did when my brain couldn't decide what was coming at me next.

Ruth climbed up on her bed and bounced on her knees. "I think Valley's making our room bigger."

"She did say she was taking measurements outside." I put my hand through the wide hole next to Ruth's bed and picked a leaf from the rhododendron bush in the garden. "You might have to sleep with me for a while. It could get too cold over where you are."

Ruth hopped down and moved her happy-face pillow to my bed.

"Listen, Ruth," I said. "You know it's a good idea to try to stay a few steps ahead of Valley."

She straightened her pillow next to mine.

"Especially when she's getting herself into a new notion." I stared at the hole in the wall. I thought about the curved scar high up on Ruth's forehead and felt sick to my stomach. She had spilled Cha-Cha Cherry Kool-Aid all over the Amish quilt Valley had been trying to sew together, and Valley must have forgotten that Ruth didn't weigh so much. It hadn't taken much of a push for Ruth's forehead to collide with the coffee table. Ruth knew better than to make Valley mad when she was working herself into a new notion. Just like when Ruth got her cast. I needed to teach her to be more careful when Valley was out of sorts.

"So what I need to do is get in her room and take a look around," I said. "I was thinking I might come across something that could help us find Ezekiel." I tried to make my shoulders relax, but the idea of going into Valley's room made them rise up next to my ears.

"Remember how Gull said her mama saves everything?" I reached over and untwisted Ruth's ribbon belt. "Well, Valley never throws anything away. Maybe we can find something with Ezekiel's address or something."

She looked at me hard when I mentioned the part about Valley's room. "We're not supposed to be touching her stuff."

I tried to act like it was no big deal. I couldn't get Ruth all riled up, because I couldn't do what I was planning without her. "All I need you to do is stand at the end of the hallway by the front door and sing something at the top of your lungs if you see Valley coming."

She didn't look at all happy about my plan, but she usually ended up doing what I said when it involved finding Ezekiel.

I left Valley's bedroom door open a wide crack, so I could make a quick escape if I needed to. My breath felt as if it was catching in my throat, and I tried not to think about what Valley might do if she caught me poking around.

It was hard to know what to look for, and I couldn't decide where to begin.

I was just starting to make my way around the room and figure out what was what when I heard the front door slam.

CHAPTER TWENTY

I THOUGHT FOR A split second about hiding, but Valley had a way of sniffing Ruth and me out, and we always ended up the worse for it.

I slipped out into the hallway, hoping she hadn't made it that far yet.

But her footsteps told me different.

"Ruth said you were back here." Gull stood nose to nose with me and looked over my shoulder, trying to see into Valley's room. Ruth was right behind her.

I let out a long, slow breath that caught in bits and pieces on the way out.

"Your living room looks like someone's taken a backhoe to it." Gull wiped at her nose with the back of her hand.

Ruth started to make the tiny beginning of a sound, like she might be getting ready to answer Gull, but she must have seen my keep-your-mouth-shut stare, because she bit her lip instead.

I rubbed my sweaty palms on the sides of my skirt. "Valley's remodeling." I wished Gull would turn around and take herself on home. I didn't know how much time I was going to have before Valley came back.

"You were in such a hurry on your way out of the class today. I couldn't catch up with you." Gull leaned one shoulder up against the wall and shifted her Hardy Boys detective story around in her back pocket.

"You read a lot of those, do you?" I pointed at the dog-eared pages and tried to will her feet to start walking toward the door.

She nodded. "I've read all but numbers five and fourteen. The records at the library say they were due back a year ago. I've been trying to get the librarian to tell me who has them." She shook her head. "But she won't give out any information, which is too bad for her. I'd even be willing to go over and get the books back."

Gull went on and on about tracking down those books, and I could see how she didn't give up once she got her mind latched on to something. Which made me think that she might be able to help me. I hated to bring in outsiders, but I wasn't having much luck with just Ruth.

"Hey, Gull," I said. "You ever try looking for anything else? Say, a lost person?" I'd have to choose my words carefully so she didn't ask too many questions. No matter how nice and helpful people were, no one ever seemed to understand about Valley.

She looked at me hard and stopped talking for about two whole seconds. So I could tell she was really interested in what I was saying. "You missing someone?"

"It's our d—" Ruth almost spilled it all up front, but I put my hand over her mouth.

I stared at Gull. "I could use your help, but I can't have you asking a lot of questions." I moved in close to her and lowered my voice to a whisper. "It makes Ruth too nervous." I raised my eyebrows. "And you've seen what happens when she gets nervous—seen *and* heard, that is."

She slid her back down the wall until she was in a low squat. "This is about that note, isn't it?"

I didn't say anything, and I squeezed Ruth's hand to remind her not to say anything, either.

"Well . . ." Gull bounced on the balls of her

feet. "Asking a lot of questions is definitely going to get you upset. So why would I do something to make you mad?" Gull shook her head. "You're pretty much the only friend I've got at this ridiculous school. I had an entire following at my old school."

I shrugged and said what I thought Mrs. Foley might say. "Give them time. They just need to get to know you."

She sighed and stood up. "All right, then. Let's get started." She pulled out her Hardy Boys book and took the lid off her pen with her teeth. "Who are we looking for?"

I released my grip on Ruth and took a deep breath. "It's Ezekiel."

Ruth rubbed at her arm. "Our daddy."

The nice thing about Gull was that she didn't even seem surprised. She had a businesslike look on her face. She narrowed her eyebrows and printed EZEKIEL with her chewed-up pen on the back page of her book.

"He's a preacher." As soon as it came out of my mouth, the worry started to bubble up in my stomach. What if that was just something Valley dreamed up as one of her notions? But then I let myself relax a little, because I heard his voice in a long-ago corner of my head, and there was no doubt about it. It was a preacher voice.

Gull put her pen behind her ear. "So I got some time. Let's head over there."

Ruth wrinkled up her nose. "Where we going?"

Gull ignored her and looked straight at me. "Come on. Time is money."

I tucked a piece of hair behind my ear and thought about all those churches we'd been visiting. "See, the thing is, that's not entirely clear. We've narrowed it down a bit, but we haven't been able to locate the exact church."

Gull's stare went from me to Ruth and back again. Then she took her pen back out. "When was the last time you saw him?"

I was little, and it was a long time ago. Ezekiel was looking for a church then. He was working on getting a place and some people to practice his preaching on. But I didn't have to think hard to remember about the last time I saw him. "I was four."

"And I was almost two." Ruth said it like she knew.

But I knew for sure. It was 1966. The year Valley remembered Christmas. It wasn't that she ever forgot completely about it. She always remembered, but it was usually a couple weeks into January.

Not the year I was four, though. She remembered right to the minute of the day. She'd even put the stand-up Santa out front a whole week ahead of time.

"The last time he was here, it was the day after Christmas," I said. "He gave me and Ruth crayons."

Ruth nodded hard, like it had just happened.

"But Ruth tried to eat hers," I said, "so I really got two boxes, and she got nothing."

Ruth had a mixed-up look, as if she was trying to decide if she was still mad or not.

He had given me something else, too. The Grand Canyon plate. But I couldn't let Ruth know it was from him. Valley didn't even know. They both thought I'd gotten it in one of my finders-keepers places. He had waited until Valley was outside in the snow with Ruth, and he'd brought it out from under the couch. "I'm going to take you girls there one day," he'd said. "We'll go right up to the edge and stare until it makes our eyes go blurry."

"So you've been looking for him for"—Gull lifted her eyes to the ceiling and counted off on her fingers—"*seven years?*"

I hated that I was giving her so much private information.

Ruth went into the voice she picked up from

Valley's old country music records. "*Valley says he's dead and gone. . . .*"

I stomped on her foot. "Shut up, Ruth!"

She gave a high squeal, still in her country music voice.

Gull blew out a low whistle. "Wow. I guess your mom really hates him."

I shot Ruth another be-quiet stare. "I got the idea to start looking for him last year when I found a box of his things in the garage." That wasn't the whole truth, but I wasn't going to tell her about Ruth's broken arm.

Gull's face lit up. "So let's see the box!"

"Can't." I shook my head. "Valley caught me with it, and she threw it away." I didn't get around to telling Gull about the picture of him in my finders-keepers car. I had the feeling I'd said far too much already.

Until Ruth opened her mouth. "That was the day I got a cast."

I couldn't believe Ruth was giving away our personal business like that. It was as if she'd lost track of what was traveling from her brain and out of her mouth.

Then Ruth suddenly seemed to come to her senses. Her eyes got all wide, and she tried to fix what she'd just said. "It was an accident," she said. "I shouldn't have been in her way."

I felt my heart speed up, because Ruth had only made things sound worse.

So I tried to change the subject. "I didn't start looking for him right away." I moved in front of Ruth, so she'd finally get the message. "I had to wait for Ruth to start riding a two-wheeler," I said. "I can't go far with her on my handlebars. It's too hard to steer. But it took her weeks to learn how to ride a bike." She cried every time she started to wobble even the tiniest bit. "Then it took another long while for her legs to get used to going very far."

Gull wrinkled up her nose at me. "Why didn't your mom just take you in the car?"

I shook my head. "She doesn't want to have anything to do with him. Once she's done with something, she's done."

Gull's eyebrows looked like I felt when I couldn't get a math problem. "So hasn't *anyone* told you anything about where he is? Hasn't anyone even *talked* about him in all this time?"

"I tried asking Aunt Dode about him again not too long ago, but she wouldn't tell me anything." I shook my head. "She just said he's gone."

Gull flipped to another page in her book. "Doesn't

he even come by to take you to Sunday dinner? Howard Crandall's mom and dad are divorced, and his dad picks him up at the top of the driveway and takes him to the diner for meatloaf every Sunday. He has the leftovers in his lunch box every Monday. You've smelled it. He sits right in back of you." She wrote something down at the top of a page in her Hardy Boys book. "It doesn't add up," she mumbled.

She fanned the pages backward. "So did he take all his stuff and everything?"

I shrugged. "He never actually lived here to begin with. So I suppose he just drove away with his Christmas presents." I'd saved up all my sticks from the Popsicles Aunt Dode kept in her freezer, and I'd made him a church. To tide him over until he could get a real one of his own.

"He had a car?" Gull perked up.

If I squeezed my eyes real tight, I could almost see the letters traveling across the back. *RAMBLER.*

"It was red."

"Now we're talking." Gull pressed down on the margin of her book with her pen. "Make and model?"

I tilted my head to the side.

"You're really making me work hard for my money here, Esther Page." She sighed like she was losing patience with me. "The car. What kind was it?"

"It was red and the hind end said *Rambler*. I know because Mr. Lang, next door, used to have one just like it. That's all I remember." It was one of the few things I was sure of when it came to Ezekiel. That and one other thing.

It was a smell, actually, but it sounded funny to say that out loud. Cherry cough drops. But I had to give Gull something to work with. So I said what I thought to be true. "He always had a cold."

Gull put the lid back on her pen and looked from me to Ruth and back again. "We'd best get going, then. Because I'm thinking I might be your last hope."

I pictured the holes Valley was making all through the house, and I was thinking Gull might be right.

CHAPTER TWENTY-ONE

I HAD TO HAND IT TO HER—Ruth took her job seriously.

She stood at the top of the hallway, near the kitchen, scanning her eyes from side to side. She was supposed to be watching and listening for any sign of Valley. A strip of sequins caught the hallway light overhead, and the sparkles kept time with the movement of her head.

I glanced at Gull and tried to unjumble my brain. "You said your mama never throws anything away," I said. "She keeps things just in case she needs to look back at them, right?"

Gull nodded. "We don't have a free bit of closet space in the house."

"I happen to know that it's the same thing with

Valley." I stepped into Valley's room on the balls of my feet, already planning how I was going to get back out.

Gull pushed around me, kicking aside Valley's ashtray with the toe of her sneaker. "At the rate you're going, you won't even make it across her room before she comes back."

She headed for the closet and pulled on the knob, folding the accordion door to the left. It caught when it was halfway open, and Gull leaned in and pushed to the side, putting all her body weight into it.

She blew out a long breath of air. "It's no use. She's got too much in there."

I reached up on tiptoe and tugged on the long chain hanging from the overhead lightbulb.

If I didn't know better, I would've thought two different people used that closet. Sweaters and blouses and skirts were divided up by color and were hung neatly on a rod, perfectly spaced. But the floor space underneath was covered with piles of boxes and a mound of plastic garbage bags stuffed full and tied shut with wide rubber bands.

Gull put her hands on her hips. "There's no rhyme or reason to this mess."

"That's Valley," I said. "There's not one bit of

rhyme or reason to her." I reached for one of the garbage bags.

Gull took the rubber band off and put it around her wrist. "We can't really take a lot out, in case we need to put it back real fast." She said it quickly and matter-of-factly, as if she was used to rifling through people's closets.

She held the bag open. "It's just clothes."

But when I put my face down in to get a better look, my breath caught in the back of my throat, because those clothes weren't Valley's. And, without warning, my mind took me back to that year when Valley remembered Christmas. "These are Ezekiel's." I pulled out a gray button-up shirt, and I remembered exactly how scratchy that wool had felt against my cheek when I hugged him. I closed my eyes and pressed the shirt hard against my forehead so I wouldn't cry in front of Gull.

Gull took a step back. "Why didn't he take his clothes when he left?" She got out her pen. "That's really weird. It was the first thing I packed when I moved out of my old house."

I curled my bottom lip up and blew out a steady breath. That always made my tears stay put. Then I tied the top back up and opened the bag next to it. "This one looks like papers."

Everything was fastened in bundles, with rubber bands looped around each little stack. "I think it's Valley's old bills." I pulled out a narrow bundle of envelopes and set it to the side. "Maybe, if I just pull a few things out, I can take it all with me to look at and try to put it back later."

"Good thinking." Gull pulled the bag open wider.

But just the thought of sneaking into Valley's room a second time made my stomach drop to the floor.

I plunged my right hand deeper and felt around in the bottom. The back of my hand caught the corner of a narrow box, and I fished it out. It was about the size of a thick picture book, and the lid was covered in green and red Christmas bells. A smashed white bow was still stuck to one corner.

I was inching the lid up, being careful not to tear anything, when Ruth sang out from the kitchen in a loud, high voice. She sang "Down in the Valley," and the words came at me fast along the hallway, in more of a screech than a melody.

"Down in the valley, the valley so low . . ."

At first I couldn't make my body do what I wanted it to. But Gull kept her wits about her. She pulled the rubber band from her wrist and fastened it back around the bag in one quick motion.

She scooped up what we'd taken out and looked at me, jerking her head toward the closet door.

I pulled the accordion door to the right with three quick tugs and followed Gull down the hall to my room.

Ruth was already in there, crouched in the corner, still humming "Down in the Valley" to the sequins along the hem of her dress.

Valley was in the living room. Or at least that's where all the noise was coming from. I could hear what sounded like a drill start up.

Gull went to take the lid off the Christmas box.

I grabbed her wrist and made her drop the box. "Not now!" I pushed it under my bed with my foot. "It's not safe here." I rubbed at my upper arm, because I could feel Valley's twist without even trying. I knew I couldn't keep Valley's things under my bed.

I hopped up on Ruth's bed and slid the window open. "Wait until I give you the signal, and then you hand everything outside to me." I took hold of Ruth's hand and looked back at Gull. "I'll hold a stick up to the window."

Gull stuck her head and shoulders in the hole by Ruth's bed. "Just hand it through right here. This is plenty wide enough."

I was a little nervous about leaving Gull in the house by herself with Valley, even for a couple of minutes. But I made myself keep going. I led Ruth out that hole and into our front yard.

CHAPTER TWENTY-TWO

THE STICK CAME OFF the little maple tree with a sharp snap, and I ran with it over my head to my bedroom window.

I hadn't needed to bother with it, because Gull already had her hands out the hole in the wall, passing everything we'd snagged from Valley's closet.

I handed the stick to Ruth and motioned Gull out. "Hurry it up!"

Valley must've worked her way into Gull's mind somehow, because Gull moved through that hole in the fastest army crawl I'd ever seen.

She grabbed one of the bundles from Ruth and raised an eyebrow at me.

I nodded toward the far side of the house. "Let's go out to the garage."

Gull turned around in a slow circle and craned her neck up. "You don't have a garage."

It was true. Most people wouldn't call it that.

I pointed to the side of the house. "It's not the kind that's attached to the house. We have to go around to the backyard."

Gull followed me but stopped short when we got through the gate, her hand on her hip.

"Come on." I went ahead, because I knew she wouldn't follow me until she'd seen that someone could actually get inside.

About two and a half of the sides of the old garage were still standing, but the rest had sunk in on itself way before I could remember.

One of the sunk-in sides had a window without the glass. That whole wall was hunched over like an old man, and the window space was practically on the ground, which made it a perfect entrance. I stepped up on a pile of wood planks and through the tilted opening into the garage.

It smelled like wet dirt and a little like the back corner of the library where they kept all the old encyclopedias that no one was allowed to check out. But that was what I liked about the garage. It was like an A to Z of Valley's life.

"What's all this stuff?" Gull climbed in the window and stared back and forth at the stacks against the back wall.

Ruth climbed in carefully after Gull, holding her skirt bunched up around her waist. "It's Valley's notion pile."

I nodded. "Every time Valley lets go of one of her notions, I drag everything out here. If I don't, the house gets too crowded." I picked up a clay pot. "This is from her gardening notion last year." I put it down beside a plastic bird-feeder made to look like the Statue of Liberty. "The only problem with that one was that it was winter, and she made her garden inside in a corner of the living room. It took me forever to get all the dirt out of there."

Gull shook her head. "You'd think we had an indoor garden, too, sometimes, what with all the dirt my brother Creed is always dragging in." She pointed at a pile of newspapers. "Hand me one of those, would you?"

I picked up the paper from the top of the stack and held it out to her. "It's from 1972. That's way last year."

Gull whisked it out of my hands. "Who cares? I'm going to sit on it, not read it."

She spread it out on the floor and plopped herself down, pulling the box with the red and green bells up onto her lap.

I narrowed my eyes at her and reached for the box, lifting one corner before she could say anything.

Ruth leaned her head over my arm and poked her nose inside. "Oh . . . it's beautiful!"

Tucked carefully into the box was a blouse. I took it out and held it up by the shoulders. It was bright peacock blue with short, puffed sleeves and tiny rhinestone buttons.

It was definitely girl clothes, but even Gull gave a little gasp.

I held it up to myself. It was way too small, and I didn't know how I knew it was meant for me. I just did.

Ruth held up a rubber-banded bundle, and I put the blouse back in the box, folding the sleeves in diagonally so it fit right.

"Undo it," I told her. "But be careful not to tear anything."

She peeled the rubber band off and set the pile down in front of her. She held up a lined note card from the top of the pile. "March" was printed in perfect teacherlike handwriting in the middle of the card.

Gull shrugged. "It's just old bills." She took a few off the top of the pile and thumbed through them.

I took them from her and looked carefully at the first one. "Maybe they have Ezekiel's name on them somewhere."

Gull tapped the corner of the envelope. "All that's here is your mom's name. 'Valley Page.'"

I flipped through the rest of them, and they were all different bills: the phone company, the electric company, and the water and garbage bills. All with Valley's name and address on them.

Ruth picked up the rest of the pile. "These are checks." She tilted her head to the side. "But they don't have Valley's name on them." She handed them to me.

"They're the kind they send back to you from the bank," Gull said. "The already used kind. My mama has about ten shoeboxes full of these things on the back porch."

"They match up with the bills." I set one in front of me and ran my finger along the bottom. "But these checks are all signed by *Leonard Butler.*"

"The only Leonard I know is the Langs' cat." I nodded toward next door. "And Ezekiel. That's what Aunt Dode calls Daddy." I could almost smell the cherry cough drop scent floating in front of my nose.

Ruth nodded slowly. "Aunt Dode never calls him Ezekiel."

Gull leaned in closer. "No address. Just his name."

I rubbed at my temples. Trying to figure Valley out gave me a headache at times. The kind that sneaks itself into the side parts of your head and hangs around for a while. And trying to figure out Ezekiel was feeling ten times worse.

Ruth held up two envelopes from the very bottom. "These aren't checks, and I don't think they're bills."

She turned them around for Gull and me to see.

The writing was slanty and very scrawly, but it was, without a doubt, my name. Mine and Ruth's.

CHAPTER TWENTY-THREE

RUTH GRABBED FOR HER envelope and lifted the flap. It was definitely a greeting card, but not one for a birthday. There was no writing on the outside— just yellow flowers spilling across the front.

She opened it, and a crisp dollar bill fell out. She scooped up the money and held it out to me. "Is this real?"

Gull raised her eyebrows. "Looks like it."

Ruth held the card open on her lap.

" 'Thinking of You.' " She read the words slowly, three times through.

I let out a shaky breath of air. "Nobody signed the bottom. The 'Thinking of You' part was already on the card when they bought it."

I pulled the card out of the "Esther" envelope. "This one's exactly the same." I felt excited and disappointed at the same time.

Gull shook her head. "Right down to the yellow flowers. And even the money."

I turned to the back, but it was blank. "Maybe they're from Valley." But even before it was out of my mouth, I knew that was impossible. I shook my head and looked at Gull. "Valley's not known for giving away money."

I started to put the card back in the envelope, but it got caught up on something. I reached inside and pulled out a piece of stiff paper, about the same size as the bookmarks the librarian gave out at school.

My hand got shaky when I read what was on the bookmark.

I turned it over and traced my finger around the church window on the back. I handed it to Gull, and she read it out loud.

"'Wheel of Ezekiel. Let us into your life.'" The voice she used wasn't her normal everyday Gull one. It was her First Methodist voice: She made her volume go from real quiet to just below a shout, without taking a breath. She was pretty good at it, too. She sounded just like the puffy preacher.

Ruth took it from Gull and tilted the church-window side up toward the light. "It looks like your garden."

The strange thing was, Ruth was right. The design on the stained-glass church window had a curve of blue glass that went up and over like the wave that I'd added to my garden. But that blue wave was outlined in thick streaks of red. Green rectangles formed a curved path along the bottom.

Ruth dropped the bookmark and grabbed the envelope from my lap and rooted around inside. She held it upside down and shook it. "That's all it said?"

I wanted it to say something else, too. "Love, Daddy," or "Love, Ezekiel," or even just his name without the "Love" part. I looked around at all the scraps and pieces of Valley's cast-off notions. There must be a way to find him.

I picked up the bookmark and pressed it between my hands. I closed my eyes and tried to make myself think of Ezekiel. I tried to remember his eyes with the slivers of green and gold in them, but they just kept coming out black and white in my mind, like they were in the picture I'd found. But when I thought real hard about him, I could almost get a touch of that smell. That cherry cough drop smell. "He's close by. I can feel it."

Ruth turned around quickly, as if she was thinking he might come sneaking up from behind.

Gull leaned back on her elbows. "Maybe Aunt Dode could use her fortune-telling to find him."

I shook my head. "Last time I asked her about him, she got mad and said I need to have a long talk with Valley. There's no way she's going to use her fortune-telling for Ezekiel."

Gull reached for the envelope that had held one of Ezekiel's cards. "I could maybe give it a shot. I saw the Amazing Kreskin do it on TV. He found a guy's lost dog."

I shrugged. It couldn't hurt to try.

Gull pressed her lips together and shut her eyes.

I started to get excited after a few minutes went by. I was hoping, from all that time she was taking, that she was zeroing in on him. "Are you getting anything?" I asked. "A street? A house number? Anything?"

"It's not going to work." Ruth said it in her singsong voice, the one she saved up for when she was in one of her know-it-all moods. She arranged her dress around her like a fan, so the light from the side windows caught up in her sequins. "He's with God."

Gull paused for a moment and opened one eye at Ruth. "You mean he's dead?" She opened her other eye and turned toward me. "You didn't say he was *that* kind of gone. Are we just wasting our time here?"

I shot Gull my best angry-Valley look. "He's not with God," I said. "He's a man of God."

Gull only closed her eyes back up halfway this time, but she moved her hands over the envelope, taking big scoops of the air.

Ruth snorted and rolled her eyes.

I was pretty sure Gull was faking, too, because she looked like Aunt Dode did when she was with her out-of-town customers. Her forehead was squished up hard, but her eyes were darting all over the place.

Gull unsquished her forehead for a second. "Give me one of those cards with the flowers on them."

She snatched it from me and pressed the card to her forehead. "It's supposed to help when you use something they've touched." She closed her eyes and squished her forehead back up, tighter than ever this time.

I leaned in and sniffed the air for cherry cough drops. "You getting anything yet?"

Ruth pulled a pretzel stick out from under her ribbon belt and started licking the salt off it. She smacked her lips together noisily, and I had to keep my elbows pressed into my sides to stop myself from belting her a good one.

Gull started to sweat, probably from all that forehead squishing she'd been doing, and she handed me back the card. "I tried to make my mind go all blank like the Amazing Kreskin, but I couldn't even do that part."

Ruth licked at her finger and picked up a clump of pretzel crumbs on her skirt.

"Where'd you get those pretzels, anyway?" Valley wouldn't buy them. She picked out only her favorite snacks, and she'd never bought pretzels of any kind. Even the ones that look like tied-up shoelaces.

Ruth pretended to smoke one as if it were a cigarette and shrugged. "I had 'em."

Gull leaned in close to me. "She probably lifted them from her teacher, Mrs. Gleason. She has a big jar of them on her desk. My sister said she munches on those things all day long."

Ruth was quick, I had to give her that. She'd probably had three or four handfuls scooped up and stashed away before Mrs. Gleason even noticed her missing from her seat.

Ruth blew out a fake puff of smoke.

Gull pushed herself to her knees. "I've got to get home and watch Wayne again." She held her Hardy

Boys book in front of me and tapped the top page. "I'm going to study these notes and draw up some charts. It's all in here, I'm sure. I just have to put it together."

I couldn't figure out what kind of charts she'd be making, but I was glad Gull wasn't a quitter.

I nodded. "Think we're closer than ever now."

Gull flipped through her book. "We don't have an address yet, but we've got a last name." She wrinkled up her forehead. "My mom has an entire shelf full of phone books. I'll make Wayne help me." She grabbed one of Ruth's stolen pretzels. "Don't worry. I won't tell him what it's for."

Ruth looked relieved to see her go.

I glared at Ruth. "You better enjoy that pretzel," I said, "because when Ezekiel gets wind of that stealing habit of yours, you might be sorry we went and found him."

I closed my eyes and pictured Ezekiel sitting on our living-room couch. It sure would be nice to have someone else to help me with Ruth.

When we got around to the front of the house, Aunt Dode was at the bottom of the driveway. Her light blue car sputtered and made wheezing noises, but she didn't turn it off, and she wasn't making any move to get out.

I waited for Gull to make her way down the street before I walked over to the driver's side.

Aunt Dode rolled down the window and handed out a foil-covered dish. "Your mama's not around, is she?"

I nodded toward the house. "She's inside." I lifted up a corner of the foil. "What's this?"

Aunt Dode kept one eye on the house. "Tuna casserole. With potato chip topping, like Ruth likes it."

Ruth smiled and reached for the dish. It was the only thing Aunt Dode knew how to make. Besides instant coffee.

"I noticed you two made off with my loaf of Wonder bread, so I thought I should bring this over." She looked toward one of the front windows. "You girls are welcome to come by, but I can't have your mother in my house anymore. I work hard for what I've got. She can't be setting fire to it all."

"Valley didn't mean to light your old place on fire." Ruth glanced back at the house. "It was the cigarette. All she did was fall asleep."

Aunt Dode put her palms up. "Whether she meant to or not doesn't matter. I'm not giving her the chance to ruin anything else."

The noisy car engine cranked up a few notches, threatening to bring Valley outside.

"You girls step back, now," Aunt Dode hollered above the noise. "Once I get this thing moving I'm never sure what it's going to do."

I took a careful step toward the house. And Valley. Because that was exactly what I had been thinking.

CHAPTER TWENTY-FOUR

"WAKE UP, ESTHER." Ruth's stale night breath blew across my face. The stuffy smell itself would have brought me out of my sleep, even if she hadn't held the flashlight right next to my forehead. "I'm cold."

I looked at my wind-up alarm clock and saw that we'd only been asleep for about an hour. The hour hand pointed to one, and a chilly breeze blew in through the hole by Ruth's bed.

"Valley's got two whole inside walls knocked out." Ruth had the skirt of her dress pulled up over her arms.

I tucked the covers around her. "It was hard to fall asleep with all that pounding and sawing she was doing."

Valley came to the doorway with a drill in her hand. "Since you girls are awake, I could use a little help." Her eyes were round, and she was doing the fast blinking that she does when she's forgotten to go to bed.

I pulled a sweatshirt over my flannel pajamas and pushed my feet into my sneakers.

She handed me a can of paint with her other hand and turned back down the hallway.

I tugged at Ruth's ribbon belt. "You sleep in that dress?"

She ignored me, which was what she always did when she didn't like the question.

"Didn't I tell you to change out of it?" I shook my head. "The bottom edges are filthy."

She licked the tips of her fingers and wiped at a section of rickrack. Then she ran off after Valley.

I bent down to tie my shoes, and I grabbed the *Charlotte's Web* and tossed it in my sock drawer, trying to make myself think like Ezekiel would. Like a preacher would. He'd probably make Ruth give it back herself. But I understood what no one else did. She couldn't help having that streak of Valley Page in her. She was just born that way. Maybe Grandma Page had passed it down to her. Just like

Valley, Ruth was only good at the taking part. She'd need to practice the giving-back part. I was sure Ezekiel could help with that.

There was something blocking my way at the end of the hallway, so I got into the living room through the bathroom, which was easy to do since there wasn't much of a wall left.

Ruth was pressed up against what looked like a gigantic sheet of white cardboard while Valley took a hammer and nails to it.

"Hold that drywall still, Ruth." Valley picked up a handful of nails from the floor. "Go get her shoes for her," she told me. "I've got a lot of sharp things around."

"Valley's putting up a whole new wall." Ruth froze her body stiff, her hands pressed to the board in front of her.

Split and shattered pieces of what used to be our house were piled and scattered everywhere. It looked as if the only thing Valley had left whole was the ceiling.

Ruth stepped on a teetery mound of wall plaster, and my heart sped up.

I put both hands to her waist to steady her. "Watch where you're stepping, Ruth!"

But Valley shot me one of her most dangerous

looks. The kind where she has half a smile but her eyes make the hair on my arms stand straight up. "At least your sister's helping," she said. "She's fine. You need to let go of her and get her shoes. If she falls, it'll be your fault for not moving fast enough."

"Just go." Ruth turned her head and whispered it into my shoulder. "I won't fall."

I moved as quickly as I could around the maze of plaster. Our house could look like our garage before I even got back with Ruth's shoes.

I went and grabbed her red rubber rain boots. "These will protect your feet better than your Keds," I said.

The new wall was blocking up where the hallway used to come into the living room.

"Help your sister hold that still." Valley glanced sideways at me. "I'm rerouting the hallway. I just have to knock out the rest of the wall between the living room and the bathroom."

"How will we get to the bathroom?" Ruth jiggled a little as if she already had to go.

"I'm just making it a little smaller." Valley pounded in the last nail and stood back to look at the new wall.

I didn't know what she was seeing, but I noticed the black cloud lifting from her face. Her eyes softened, and her voice took on the even, easygoing tone she got when she was discovering a possibility. I could almost see the broken pieces forming something new and whole in her mind.

She handed Ruth and me each a hammer. "I'll need your help getting the rest of the other wall down. Those last boards are giving me a hard time."

Ruth smiled real big and took her hammer to the wall.

I swung mine lightly at first, but then I got into the rhythm of it. And when Valley switched on the radio, I made my hammer hit in time with the music.

Vicki Lawrence came on, and Valley cranked it up. I loved it when she sang with the radio. She could make her voice sound just like Vicki's.

I knew all the words to "The Night the Lights Went Out in Georgia," and I turned my voice up, trying to make it sound like Valley's, all clear and a little twangy.

Ruth tried to sing with us, too, but she always got the words mixed up. Usually that annoyed me, but tonight was different. It felt like a party, with all that singing and hammering.

But even with the smashing and singing, that

note managed to work its way into my mind. Valley could be like your favorite birthday party when you took away the sharp edge of her. But it would be a birthday party I could never invite any friends to.

I thought about Mrs. Foley trying to get in touch with Valley, and all the worry crawled back into my brain. And Mrs. Foley was going to ask me again if Valley had read the note. There was no way I could let Valley go down to the school when she was like this.

I felt my ears heat up when I imagined my teacher trying to keep up with Valley's fast sentence spurts and trying to make sense of her halfway words.

The radio said it was three-thirty when we were finally smashing away at the last board.

"This remaining two-by-four is stubborn!" Valley wiped at her forehead.

I gave the count of three, and all of us smashed our hammers at it together.

When we finally got it out, Valley let go of her handle and gathered us close to her in a tight hug. "What would I do without my girls?" She took our tools and dropped them beside hers. "Now, you two go get some rest. You've got school in the morning, and I've got some painting to do!"

My arms and shoulders ached as Ruth and I flopped into my bed. But I didn't mind one single bit. I pulled the covers up around Ruth, and I closed my eyes and listened to Valley's voice blend in with Mick Jagger and the Rolling Stones, trying to push Mrs. Foley and the note out of my mind.

CHAPTER TWENTY-FIVE

WHEN I WOKE UP, my eyelids felt heavy all the way down to my eyelashes, and I had a fuzzy feeling like my brain hadn't nudged itself awake yet.

I looked at my clock and thought I was reading the numbers wrong. But when I moved closer, I could see I had slept through morning recess and then some. The cooks would be setting up their lunch cart in the hallway about now. My stomach turned over because I knew that meant more nosy teacher questions if we walked in now. I was just too tired to come up with some good answers.

Ruth slept flat on her back with her mouth wide open, a bundle of hot pink and glittery sequins, her ribbon belt dangling over the side of the bed.

I nudged her with my toe, and her eyes peered

up at me. "I couldn't get to sleep," she said. "The popping was keeping me awake."

"Valley was just painting," I said. "You need to teach yourself to sleep through the loud parts of her notions. She saves up her sleep, but you and me can't do it the way she does.

"And, speaking of sleep, we slept all the way through morning recess and into math. By the time we'd get there, it would be practically time to turn around and go back home again." I tried to fluff out her bangs where they'd clumped up in the middle of her forehead. "Which is a good thing, because you need a good long bath."

"I was going to take one last night," Ruth said. "Before we went to bed the second time. But I was too tired. And Valley turned off the water in the bathroom. Probably when she knocked out the wall."

I finger-combed the back of her hair. "Well, we're going to have to get you cleaned up somehow before tomorrow. We don't need another note on top of the one we've already got." The thing was, I was going to have to come up with a good enough note for both of us. I would have to give it some thought when I wasn't so tired. And I'd take my time with Valley's signature until it was perfect.

Which reminded me. I was going to need to get

more supplies for my relief map. Maybe, if I could impress Mrs. Foley enough with my project, she'd forget about the note for a while.

"Go make us each a butter-and-sugar sandwich, please, Ruth," I said. "We're going on a finders-keepers trip."

Valley wasn't in her room, and she was nowhere to be seen when I walked through what used to be the bathroom wall into the living room. But her paint cans were dry, and her brush sat by itself on top of a broken-off piece of wall. The room had that quiet kind of empty feeling that made me both sad and a little nervous at the same time.

Ruth limped up behind me and handed me a sandwich thick with butter. "I had to use the end pieces," she said. "It's all that was left."

"Valley must have gone to get more paint." I took a bite out of my sandwich. "Why are you limping?"

She sat down on a paint can and stuck out her foot. "I think I stepped on something."

"Does it hurt?" I bent down so I could see it better.

She nodded, the corners of her eyes tearing up, as if I had just reminded her to cry. "I was afraid you'd be mad, because I forgot to put my boots back on."

"It'll be fine." I took my fingernails to a jagged splinter of wood and plucked it out.

She let out a puppy yelp.

"Go wash it." It was best to do those kinds of things quickly with Ruth.

She limped off to the kitchen, and I tried to pick up anything that looked sharp.

"Don't come back in here!" I yelled toward the kitchen. "I'm bringing your boots to you."

She was sitting down at the kitchen table when I dropped her rubber boots in front of her. She held up her foot. "The purple stuff won't wash off."

I sat next to her and brought her foot up on my lap. "That's just a bruise, I think. Put on your boots, and I'll see if Ford has a Band-Aid when we get to the vacant lot."

She started to walk out the front door, but I grabbed her arm and steered her toward the back. "We can't let Mrs. Lang see us. It's a school day, remember?"

We went the back way to the vacant lot. It was a shortcut you could take only if you weren't on your bike, because we had to go over lots of grass. "Remember to stay along the fence when we cut through someone's yard," I said. "And what do you say if someone yells at us to get off their property?"

Ruth rolled her eyes and tried to make her voice sound like mine. "We're looking for our dog that ran away."

"How come your dress looks so heavy?" I watched her reach under her sweatshirt and hitch the top up.

"It's wet." She lifted the bottoms of the skirt up and out to the sides.

"What?" I could see it drop heavily when she let go.

"You said it was dirty, so I washed it with Mr. Bubble in the kitchen sink." She lifted up a corner and blew on it, flapping it up and down in the air.

"You're going to have to wear something else sooner or later," I said.

She kept lifting up different sections and flapping them. Then she swung her pocketbook in a figure eight and pretended she hadn't heard me.

Ruth usually switched her pocketbooks, sometimes more than once a day, but for the past couple of days I'd noticed only the shiny pink one from the Goodwill bin. Every time she made a figure eight, a couple of silver stars would fall off. They were the big lick-and-stick kind. The kind you could only get at school. I was pretty sure regular people couldn't buy them. Only teachers.

"Where'd you get those stars, Ruth?" I picked one up from the ground and held it in front of her.

She shrugged. "Found 'em."

I thought about the *Charlotte's Web*, and my stomach gave a little jump. I had to get that back to her teacher somehow. I patted my pouch, feeling for the sharp corner of the note, and I tried to make my mind settle down.

As we got closer to the finders-keepers place, I could hear a couple of loud voices.

I grabbed Ruth's arm. "Those are angry, arguing voices, and I think one of them is Ford's."

Ruth tipped her head to the side and listened. "Only one of the voices is angry. Ford's voice is calm. It's an explaining voice, like Mrs. Gleason has."

But when we got to the hole in the fence, both voices had quieted down, and the only person I could see was Ford, prying the door handle off one of the upside-down cars.

"You got a Band-Aid?" Ruth went right up to him and pulled her boot off.

He set the door handle on the ground and sat down in the dirt next to her. "They let school out early today?"

I nodded, but I could tell by the way he wrinkled his nose that he didn't believe me.

He brought Ruth's foot up to his face. "What happened here?"

I was surprised he was that close to Ruth's foot. I wanted to plug my own nose when I thought about the rubber-boot smell.

Ruth shrugged. "Stepped on a wood splinter. Valley's remodeling."

"You show this to your mom?" He squinted his eyes at it.

Ruth shook her head. "She wasn't home."

Ford opened his mouth as if he was getting ready to say something, but he couldn't make the words come out.

"What's wrong?" I bent down next to Ruth's foot. My stomach felt a little queasy when I saw Ford's face. "Is her foot worse than I thought?"

"No, it's fine. It looks like she got all of the splinter out." He helped her pull her boot back on and put his face down even with hers. "Is your mom gone a lot?"

I stepped to the other side of her and held my breath.

CHapter Twenty-six

I KEPT MY BREATH INSIDE until Ruth finally said no. She knew better than to answer any questions about Valley.

And then I almost hugged Ruth when she went and changed the subject. "Who were you arguing with?" She lifted up her leg and wiggled the toe of her boot at Ford.

"It was just a customer." Ford rolled his eyes. "She was trying to pay me less than we'd agreed on. Even though I fixed her engine perfectly."

Ruth stomped her good foot. "Why didn't you just yell back at her?"

Ford pressed his lips together and shook his head. "My mother always taught me you shouldn't burn your bridges."

Ruth shook her head. "I would have told her to get lost."

"Not a good idea," he said. "I want her to leave here happy. I want her to tell her friends and neighbors about me, so I'll get more customers at my shop."

Maybe that was what Valley had done with Ezekiel. Burned her bridges. Maybe Ezekiel had done like Aunt Dode and declared himself Valley-free.

I should've known better than to think Ruth would just drop the whole subject. "Valley burned her bridges, didn't she?" I'd been distracted by some green glass on the ground behind me, so I was too late to stop her before she opened her mouth again. "When she burned down Aunt Dode's place, she burned her bridges, didn't she?"

"Your mom burned a place down?" He brought his face right in front of Ruth's again, so she couldn't look away.

"Ruth has her facts all mixed up. You know how little kids are." I thought fast. "Valley told us we were going to burn the house down if we left the stove burners on again." I grabbed Ruth's hand and pulled her to her feet. We needed to get out of there before she said anything else.

He talked toward the ground, and his voice was

so low I could barely hear him at first. "When I left to move back here, my mom told me to look in on you two."

Ford wasn't making any kind of sense. "Your mom asked you to look in on *us*? Me and Ruth?"

He nodded. "When I was getting ready to move back here a little over six months ago. She gave me some money to help me start my car-repair business." He picked up the door handle. "I tried to get her to come with me, but she said no. She said she'd had enough of this place years ago, and she was happy where she was."

"What does your car-repair business have to do with me and Ruth?" It felt like having a conversation with Valley when she was out of sorts. You had to try and fit the bits and pieces together in a logical order.

"It doesn't have anything to do with you." He shook his head as if we were the ones not making any sense. "My mom told me about you and your mother, and she said to look in on you."

"Your mom knows Valley?" Ruth took her boot back off and wiggled her toes.

"My mom knew her a long time ago." Ford pulled a tool out of his pocket and got to work prying another door handle off. "Doesn't care for her much. But she told me to see if you two girls were okay."

I didn't need any more people asking about us or Valley. Especially people who didn't care for her much. "Well, as you can see for yourself, we're fine." Then I reminded myself to be polite. "Tell her thanks for asking."

And even though this was supposed to be a finders-keepers trip, I led Ruth back out through the hole in the fence.

It was hard to hurry a person who was limping, especially when she had too-big rubber boots on. And I made her get away from Ford and the finders-keepers place a lot faster than I probably should have.

"What were you thinking?" I squeezed her hand a little harder than I should have, too. "Since when have we ever given away Valley's personal business to someone? And you heard what he said! His mama doesn't even like Valley."

Then she started to cry, which just plain made me mad.

I dropped her hand and stayed ahead a few steps, which I knew would make her upset, but I'd had enough of her. All I'd wanted was to have a nice afternoon collecting.

By the time we got home, I decided I wasn't going to let the day completely go to waste. I'd go in my room and put together some more plans for my relief-map project.

"I want to paint a little." Ruth sat on the floor in the living room and picked up Valley's brush. She swished the tip of it over the underside of a paint-can lid. "There's still a tiny bit left," she said. "It should be enough to do some cat whiskers."

"Have at it." I kicked another lid toward her. "Just don't use the one by the couch. That's where Valley was putting all of her cigarette butts."

I made my way back to my room, and I was just taking the lid off the box of supplies from Mrs. Foley when I started hearing the popping. But I couldn't exactly tell where it was coming from. Then I remembered what Ruth had said when we woke up. "The popping was keeping me awake," she'd told me.

It sounded as if it was up high somewhere. I tried to follow the noises, but it was hard, because they'd stop for a while, then they'd start up again, two or three in a row. It was beginning to get on my nerves, and I couldn't concentrate on my project, so I went to get the plug-in radio.

Ruth was already listening to it, painting her cat

whiskers on the new wall while Neil Young sang about a heart of gold. But she must have known she had gotten on my last nerve, because she didn't say a word when I unplugged it and took it back to my room with me.

I changed it to my favorite station, the one that Valley listened to. Then I knew my day was turning itself around, because Melanie came on singing "Brand New Key."

I was wishing for a brand-new pair of roller skates just like Melanie's when I heard the cracking.

And Ruth's scream.

Chapter Twenty-seven

"RUTH!" I SCREAMED. The house was completely silent. And still.

I couldn't see much of anything except the chunks of ceiling and swirls of dust.

"Ruth! Please answer me!" I stood by the toilet in the bathroom and looked for a sparkle of a sequin or a rubber boot.

My stomach heaved, but I made myself ignore it. I didn't have time to be sick. "Ruth! I'm not mad anymore! Please come out!"

Then I turned in a slow circle and froze. Because I'd seen something pink. Something pink and shiny. Just past a wide pile of ceiling pieces.

I was afraid to move closer, but I had to.

And then I heard her. "Esther?" A soft, squeaky

voice in the middle of all that stillness. That whisper caused a flood of relief to travel down to my legs, making them rubbery and wobbly to walk on.

I headed toward the couch and the pink pocket-book with the lick-and-stick stars.

I couldn't believe a person could fit into such a tiny space, but there was Ruth, all folded up and wedged between the couch and the living-room wall.

"My voice wouldn't work." She reached out and grabbed the handle of her pocketbook.

"Are you okay?" I touched her boot. "Are you hurt?" I wanted to pull her close to me, but I was afraid to make anything worse.

"I thought my voice was hurt for a while there." She pulled her pocketbook onto her lap. Her hair and the tops of her shoulders were covered in white ceiling dust.

"It's because you were frightened." My whole body was scared, and no matter how hard I tried, I couldn't stop shaking. "The ceiling crash pushed your voice right out of you."

"I can see the attic." Ruth looked up toward the big hole over the bathroom. It smiled at us real wide, like one of those scary circus clowns.

"I guess Valley took down too much wall." I

hugged myself. "We need to get out of here in case something else comes down."

Ruth's eyes got round. "We can't leave until Valley gets back."

She was right. Valley always forgot to pay attention. I took Ruth's hand and helped her stand up. "It will be dark soon, and the overhead light came down with the chunks of ceiling. Valley could wander in and end up right under the weak part."

Ruth looped the long handle of her pocketbook over her shoulder.

"We have to wait outside," I said. "Out front where we can watch for Valley's truck."

She started to walk toward the bathroom.

I yanked her back by the handle of her pocketbook. "What are you doing? We can't go that way!"

I led her in the opposite direction, into the kitchen, and grabbed what was left of Aunt Dode's tuna casserole out of the refrigerator. "Get some plates and spoons." I pointed at the silverware drawer. "And fill the Kool-Aid pitcher with water. I think Aunt Dode used a whole bag of potato chips on top."

She put two plates and some silverware in her pocketbook.

"Never mind the glasses. We can just drink right from the pitcher."

"What if I have to go to the bathroom?"

I had to admit, since my shakes were slowing down, I had to go myself. "We can go behind the tree in the side yard. If you can't wait until it gets dark, we can be a lookout for each other."

We went outside to the rock garden in front of our room. I stood at the edge of the swirl I'd made with the blue glass, and it made me remember Ezekiel's card. *Wheel of Ezekiel. Let us into your life.*

I thought about Ruth behind that pile of ceiling pieces, and Ezekiel just seemed so far away from us. Fathers were supposed to stick around and take care of their kids. They were supposed to make sure nothing bad came down on them.

When I stood back on a patch of grass and squinted my eyes up at the roof, I couldn't see anything out of the ordinary. "There's not a scratch on the outside, Ruth. It's as if the inside part never happened."

"I'm hungry." Ruth lifted a corner of foil from Aunt Dode's dish and took a pinch of broken-up potato chips. "They're not crunchy anymore, but they're still really good."

"Let's sit down," I said. "We can have a picnic." We sat cross-legged on the grass with the dish between us.

The picnic was fun at first. Until it started to get chilly. And dark. As the sun began to go down, Ruth got real quiet. I could see her hands opening and closing, forming small shaky fists.

"Listen, Ruth." I put the foil back on the dish and sealed it up tight. "Valley should be home pretty soon."

Ruth picked up one of her fallen stars out of the grass and licked the back, trying to make it stick again along the bottom edge of her pocketbook. "I want to go inside."

"I don't think it's safe, Ruth."

But it was getting so cold. "I'll go in and grab some blankets." I could be in and out of there in a couple of minutes. My mouth got really dry, but I convinced myself it would be fine.

I went headfirst through the hole in our wall. And when I got my shoulders and arms in, I could hear the radio. It was still on, which seemed so strange. It had felt as if the whole world had been turned off when I'd heard the ceiling crash. I made myself picture Ruth in the corner. Safe. Instead of what could have happened.

I tried to keep my ears trained on the living room. I wanted to be able to get out of there fast if something started to fall, and I kept imagining I heard popping sounds.

I fed my project and both our bedspreads through the hole to Ruth. Then I grabbed her book and a flashlight and climbed out.

"You can help me finish sketching my relief map." I really didn't want her to help, but I had to keep her busy while we waited for Valley.

"We could go get Ford," she said. "If he's good at fixing cars, he could fix our ceiling, for sure."

In that quick second I remembered why I'd been mad at her in the first place. "You've told Ford enough already." Part of me wanted to go get him, though. Because who knew how Valley was going to take care of it?

I draped one of the bedspreads across two bushes, making us a cozy fort. "Look here, Ruth." I showed her the peephole I'd left. "No one can see us over here, and we can still see Valley when she pulls up."

I made a little nest with the other blanket, turned on the flashlight, and read the stolen *Charlotte's Web* to Ruth until she fell asleep.

Chapter Twenty-eight

I TRIED MY HARDEST to wait up for Valley. I even made myself sing all the verses of "This Old Man" six times, but my body was too tired.

When I woke up, Ruth was reaching out through the opening in the blanket, getting a long drink from the water pitcher. "Valley's truck is not in the driveway."

"Are you sure?" I poked my head out. "You're right. She's not parked out front at the curb, either."

I wiped at a dribble of water on Ruth's chin. "It's early, Ruth," I said. "We have to get you cleaned up, and we need to go to school." I thought about Gull. "Someone's bound to come looking for us if we don't show up again today."

She licked her thumb and wiped at some old ceiling dust on her knee. "What about Valley?"

"It's light out now," I said. "She'll be able to see the ceiling for herself."

If we were really careful and kept our ears open for the popping sound, we could use the kitchen. I couldn't send Ruth to school without wiping her down.

I picked up Aunt Dode's tuna casserole and led Ruth into the kitchen. "I'll put this in the fridge, and we can have the rest for dinner tonight. Maybe I can trade someone some of my school lunch for a few fresh potato chips to put on top."

I plugged up the sink and put in a big squirt of dishwashing liquid. "Climb in, Ruth." I slid the kitchen chair over. "And take that dress off. Everybody in the world will know something's up if you try to wear that filthy thing to school."

"I could wash it again." She reached toward the dishwashing liquid.

I pushed it out of her reach. "I said no."

I could tell she didn't want to, but she took it off. She draped it carefully over the back of one of the chairs, as if it was a real Cinderella gown.

She fit most of the way into the sink, but I knew

I wouldn't. I washed my hair in the sink, but I had to give the rest of myself a good wipe-down next to it.

"I forgot to bring our clean clothes with us, so we'll have to put our dirty ones back on till we get to our room." I hated to hand her that filthy dress, but I had no choice. Valley's orange dish towels were great for drying off, but they were way too small to wrap yourself in.

I was going to make Ruth wait next to the hole outside while I went in to grab our clothes, but she crawled in before I could stop her. A sleeve with a mother-of-pearl button hung over the bottom drawer of my dresser. I pulled out the cowboy shirt and held it up. It was a nice light brownish-white color, like the thick layer of cream that swam across the top of Aunt Dode's coffee. It seemed even more beautiful than when Ruth had pulled it out of the Goodwill bin. The buttons looked as if they were made of white-and-pink swirly marble with a thin gold rim. I shook it out and put it on.

I could tell by the way her top lip curled up that Ruth was jealous. Then I remembered about the other one. I pulled it from my drawer, but when I held it out to her, I saw she was already putting something on.

It was the peacock-blue blouse with the short, puffed sleeves. The one from the Christmas box in

Valley's closet. The one I thought we'd hidden out in the garage.

She buttoned up the rhinestone buttons and smoothed down the front with the palms of her hands.

"Ruth!" I shook my head. "You'd better not let Valley see you wearing that. She'll know we've been in her closet!"

She reached for her long-sleeved sweatshirt and pulled it on so it hung almost to the middle of her pink skirt with the tiny red roses all over it. "I'll take it off before I leave school."

I was just happy she hadn't insisted on putting the dress back on, so I decided to leave her alone.

I pulled on my purple corduroy skirt and rolled up the bottoms of the sleeves on my cowboy shirt. It was a little big, but it looked fine. I lifted my arm up to my nose and sniffed. It still had a little bit of the back-of-the-refrigerator smell from the Goodwill bin, but that would probably wear off when the fresh air got to it.

I grabbed my relief-map plans and stuffed the quilt in the hole behind us. "Don't want anything wandering in from the garden when we're gone."

We were almost at school when my stomach started rumbling. I had been so nervous going back in the house, I hadn't even felt hungry. The one thing that I wished for was something warm to take the edge off. Like a toasted cheese sandwich. The Ezekiel kind with just the perfect amount of melty cheese and butter.

Gull was waiting for me at the edge of the playground when we got to school. "Where were you yesterday?" She thumbed through her Hardy Boys book.

"Go on and catch up with your class." I pushed Ruth toward the line by the swings.

"We had appointments. Ruth and me had to go to the dentist." I saw Ruth glance back at me as I said it, and I couldn't look in Gull's direction at all. Number one, I felt guilty lying, because I liked her, and, number two, she was a really good detective. The minute she looked me in the eye, she'd start asking questions.

"You do realize we're now a day behind, don't you?" Gull grabbed a comb out of her back pocket and took a swipe at her spiky bangs. "I spent an hour or so going over my notes yesterday." She thumbed through her book. "And there are too many things that don't add up with this Ezekiel guy. I'm coming up with a whole lot of nothing." She bent down so her eyes were staring straight into mine. "Which is doubly weird because I'm a trained detective. I *always* get things to add up."

I tried to look away, but she stared even harder.

"I'll be by tonight." She moved into the fifth-grade line. "I've jotted down quite a few questions."

That was when I really got nervous. I'd have to try to keep her outside, in the yard. "How about I come by *your* house?"

She shrugged and followed the line up the steps and into the school. "I guess you could. You'll probably end up helping me watch the kids. Soon as someone sets foot in our house, Mama puts them to work." She made her way to her desk, because Mrs. Foley was giving her the evil eye. Mrs. Foley was almost as good as Valley when it came to drilling her eyes into someone.

She gave me a different kind of eye when she walked toward my desk. She put a paper facedown in the corner in front of me, and from the way her eyebrows went up, I knew that had to be my spelling test. The one from Monday. I could see the red pen bleeding on through from the other side. I didn't even have to turn it over to see the thick six and tall zero up toward the top. She wouldn't have even had to write the "See Me" next to it. I knew better than anyone. Anything below a seventy-five always had a "See Me" next to it.

"Mrs. Foley?" I felt the edge of the sandwich in my desk. "I know you are going to want me to see you after school, but I have an appointment. The seeing you is going to have to wait until tomorrow."

She pressed her lips together so they made a perfectly straight line. That mouth of hers looked angry, and I could have been mistaken, but I thought her eyes had a sad tinge to them. "You can come in tomorrow." She tilted her head down, bringing herself a little closer to me. "Before school. I'll be here early."

Mrs. Foley's shoes stayed next to my desk for a while, as if she had more to say. But then she took a deep breath and went on to the next row with her spelling papers.

Gull was tapping out a quick little drumbeat back and forth from her desk to her lap, so I knew she had gotten a hundred, or at least something in the nineties.

I'd have to do a bit more paying attention. Valley had never looked very long or hard at my report cards, but somehow I knew Ezekiel would. He'd probably want to see them all right up front. He'd want to be filled in on everything he'd missed since he'd last seen us. Being a preacher, he'd be worried about people doing the right thing. And studying your spelling words was sure to be one of them.

I tried to clear my mind and get ready to listen to Mrs. Foley, but Bradley Norris kept humming "The Lion Sleeps Tonight." As usual, he was pitch-perfect with each one of his notes, which actually tended to make things worse. It made you forget what you were doing and hum along with him.

Mrs. Foley moved through the morning like a bulldozer. She was always saying she needed to be getting us ready for sixth grade, but it was only October, and I was still trying to get my mind used to fifth.

My stomach growled, and I unwrapped my sandwich in my desk, which was difficult to do with one hand. And it was wrapped in stiff waxed paper that crinkled loudly when I touched it. But it was chicken-cutlet day, and I couldn't wait. Mrs. Foley's chicken-cutlet sandwiches were like they were straight out of a restaurant. It was always hard to save half for Ruth. I bent down by my desk and took a few little bites.

I wished things wouldn't go so fast after lunch recess. I wanted the afternoon to last forever. As soon as I left, I'd have to go back home and try to fix all that was broken. But at school I could keep working on my relief map. And when Mrs. Foley called me up to her desk toward the end of the day, I'd almost convinced myself that she was going to suggest that I stay after the going-home bell and keep working on it. She'd probably figured out by now that big projects were my specialty.

But it wasn't me she wanted to talk about. It was Ruth.

She used her quiet teacher voice. The one where the other kids couldn't hear what she was saying. I appreciated that, because it turned out she wanted to talk about the note. That same note that was still in my suede pouch, hanging over my shoulder.

"I tried to call your mother at lunch." Mrs. Foley leaned in and made her eyes line up with mine.

"It's pretty busy down at the phone company," I said. "It'll probably take them at least a week before they turn our phone back on again."

"I don't normally do this"—Mrs. Foley looked as if she was starting to change her mind—"but I have seen how well you take care of your sister. I know you are a responsible girl. You've shown your-self to be very mature for a fifth-grader."

She seemed to want to talk about Ruth, not Valley, so I held my pouch tightly to my side and made myself take a deep breath.

"Ruth's teacher has some concerns, and she really needs to talk to your mother. Mrs. Gleason tried to give Ruth notes to take home on a number of occasions. But she kept finding them crumpled up in the back of Ruth's desk." Her eyes went up to the ceiling as if she were searching for the right thing to say. "I was hoping that, if you could tell your mother how concerned we all are, we could get the ball rolling faster. Ruth can't see the school counselor without your mother's permission."

"The school counselor?" We didn't need anyone else nosing around in our business. Who knew what Ruth might say?

Mrs. Foley leaned in so close, I could smell the wintergreen mints she always kept in her desk. "Ruth is young. We all feel that the sooner we nip this stealing of hers in the bud, the better chance she has of shaking such a bad habit."

I must have looked as if I didn't understand her, because she kept talking. "Surely you and your mother have noticed that Ruth comes home with things that don't belong to her."

Of course I had noticed it, and Gull had, too. But no adults had ever said anything about it. Until now.

"Anyway, Esther"—she tried to smile at me, but it wasn't her you-are-doing-a-good-job smile; it was more like an I-feel-sorry-for-you smile—"please let your mother know how important it is that she contact Ruth's teacher."

I was sure she looked right at my pouch when she said it. I walked to my desk and tried to ignore Gull. She was so anxious to find out what was happening that she was practically falling out of her chair.

But I refused to look up. I pretended to search for something in my desk, trying to make my thoughts stop crashing into one another. I knew Ruth's stealing had gotten out of hand. Especially when I found out about the *Charlotte's Web*. And the note meant they wanted Valley to help.

Prickly sharp pains were starting up in the middle of my forehead, like a kind of warning. I didn't even know where Valley was. And when she did come back, how would I settle her down enough to go to a meeting at school?

When the bell rang to go home, I knew there was no holding Gull back. I tried to get out the door as fast as I could, but Gull was already there, blocking my way. "What is going on?" She hooked her arm through my elbow and pulled me out to the playground with quick giant steps.

"Nothing," I said. "What do you mean?" Even I didn't believe the words that were coming out of my mouth.

She led me toward the jungle gym and planted her feet in the playground sawdust so we were toe to toe. "I've never heard of a dentist appointment that lasts all day."

"I can't get into it right now, Gull." Quickly I scanned the handful of kids that were still milling around the playground, and I didn't see any sign of a pink pocketbook with lick-and-stick stars.

"You haven't seen Ruth, have you?" I looked toward the side door where she usually came out.

Gull shook her head. "Not since this morning. Just before school."

"Wait here in case she comes out. I'll be right back." I retraced her usual steps back to her classroom. But when I got there, all I saw was her teacher, Mrs. Gleason, packing up her papers and such to go home.

"Can I help you?" She grabbed her sweater and picked up her bag. "Did you come for Ruth's homework?"

"Her homework?" I looked toward the coat closet, but Ruth was nowhere in sight.

Mrs. Gleason's eyes went to the clock over the door, and I could see she was in a hurry. "It's on her desk. Everything she missed." She started for the door. "Since she missed all afternoon, she can have an extra day to make it up."

"She missed all afternoon?" I couldn't make sense of what she was saying.

"Yes, of course, dear," she said. "She left for a dentist appointment right before lunch." Mrs. Gleason stopped at the door and looked back at me. "Please tell her we can have our little talk tomorrow morning instead."

Ruth had never been one to face up to things when she was in trouble. I thought of what Mrs. Foley had said about her stealing. If Ruth knew they were on to her, there was one thing I knew for absolute sure: She wasn't coming back to school anytime soon.

Chapter Twenty-nine

GULL WAS SITTING at the very top of the monkey bars when I came back out. "You can see for about a mile from up here. And I haven't seen any sign of your sister."

"You probably won't, either." I shaded my eyes with my hand and looked up at her. "Turns out she got a pretty good head start."

"She's probably just gone home." Gull climbed down slowly, each foot feeling carefully for the bar below before she stepped on it. She reached the ground and brushed some sawdust off the pocket of her Boy Scout shirt. "My brother Creed's got a temper that goes right through him, kind of like Ruth. If Creed's mad about something, or in trouble, he hides out under the old rabbit hutch in the back corner of the yard. Mama just lets him stew until it burns itself out. Then he comes in and has his dinner, and he's fine."

"I'm not sure if she's mad about something," I said, "but she's definitely in trouble."

Gull nodded. "I figured so. They find out about the *Charlotte's Web*?"

I headed toward the sidewalk. "Looks like it."

"Mrs. Gleason really likes that book, so I knew it was just a matter of time before she tracked it down." Gull stopped to tie her shoe.

"Turns out that's what the note was about." I patted my suede pouch.

"I'll come by later," she said. "Right now I've got to babysit while Mama does her grocery shopping." She waved her Hardy Boys book in the air in front of her. "Me and Wayne didn't come up with anything in the phone directory, but we're not done yet. My mom's got a whole pile of the surrounding counties." She ran off down the sidewalk, taking giant leaps over each crack.

I picked my feet up, too. I needed to give Ruth a good talking to. I wanted to have the stealing thing about cleared up before we found Ezekiel. I didn't want that to be the first thing we had to talk about.

But when I got home, Valley's truck was still

gone, and Ruth was nowhere to be found. I don't know how to explain it, but things just didn't feel right. I got that same prickly feeling on the backs of my arms that I got the other day when I woke up. The day she was missing.

I don't think I even breathed until I got into the living room. But it was just the way we'd left it in the morning, all the way down to the dusty pile of ceiling chunks. I let out my breath and tried to will my heart to slow back down.

And there wasn't one tiny sign that she'd been in the kitchen. Not even a snack wrapper or a sock.

Ruth always did everything in the exact same order. She came in the door and walked a few feet in and sat down. Then she took off her shoes and socks and emptied out the sawdust from the playground. After that, she always checked on her stuffed animals in our room. She rearranged them every afternoon so they didn't get stiff necks.

But when I went across the front yard, Ruth's quilt was plugging up the hole, exactly as I'd left it that morning.

Then I remembered what Gull had said about Creed hiding under the rabbit hutch out back.

I ran around to the backyard and did a quick lap. "Ruth?" I called her name in every corner. "No one is mad at you, I swear!" I stopped at the garage and bent down to look in the window. "Ruth? You in there?" I climbed in and sifted through Valley's notion pile. No Ruth.

It was looking more and more as if Ruth had done a runner.

I leaned up against the garage and tried to pretend I was in her head. She didn't like a whole lot of change. I knew that about her. She'd hated getting left at the Mark and Pack, so I knew she'd never go back there. There was only one other logical place to find her.

I hopped on my bike and tried to make myself pedal slowly, because she could blend right into the background when she wanted to.

I scanned the corners of each and every yard along the way, but there was absolutely no sign of Ruth.

Just before the vacant lot, as the road came to an end, I passed a tiny cemetery on my right. I took an extra-deep breath for Ruth and remembered how she always took three or four cheater breaths before our feet found the dirt and the broken-up macadam at the fence opening to Ford's property.

I went to our car in the back of the lot, and I knew for certain she'd been there, because Ezekiel's picture was gone. All that was left on the door of the glove compartment was a torn corner of masking tape.

I stood in the very middle of the vacant lot and turned in a slow circle, looking for footprints, anything that would tell me where Ruth had gone. My head was getting a dull ache right behind my eyes. The only thing I could think of to do was to try to retrace her steps.

Ford lived next door to the vacant lot, but I'd never been there before. I looked through an opening in the fence slats. I could see a tiny yellow house and a rickety brown barn. The barn was definitely Ford's auto-body shop, because I could see the red truck parked next to it.

I made my way across what used to be a yard, where the grass had forgotten about growing, stepping carefully around thick, muddy patches of chocolatey dirt.

Next to the barn were pieces of cars. Not the sad and broken kind, like the doll parts at the bowling alley. Ford's pieces were shiny and colorful and waiting to be a part of something again. It would be just like Ruth to hide herself in the middle of it all.

I was listening for any whisper of her when I heard a radio playing. Three Dog Night was singing about Jeremiah being a bullfrog. When I poked my head through the opening in the barn door, something rattled a far-back corner of my brain.

It took a while for my thoughts to sort themselves out. There was only one car inside the barn. The hood was open, and Ford leaned over the front, the whole top half of his body disappearing into the engine. Seeing the car started my thoughts swirling, but it was the side wall of the barn that made my whole body freeze up.

CHAPTER THIRTY

FORD WIPED AT A SMUDGE of oil on his cheek with the side of his hand. "I wondered when you were going to show up."

"What are you doing with that car?" I stared at the back end of the red Rambler.

He ignored me in a very Ruth-like way and turned down his radio. "Your sister was here." He leaned back on the car. "I caught her trying to sneak my cat out in one of those giant pocketbooks she's always carrying." He waved a rag toward the striped orange cat asleep in the back window.

I ran my hand along a wooden bench next to the car. But I could see that it wasn't a normal old sitting bench. There were three or four of them in different shades of brown resting against one another, with car parts piled high on the seats.

Ruth and I had been going on our finders-keepers trips to the vacant lot for a year, and the Wheel of Ezekiel had been practically under our noses. I went to the stained-glass window propped up against the side wall and traced my pointer finger over the cobalt-blue glass that went up and over like the tip of a wave.

My heart felt as if it was going to thump out of my chest. "Where is he?" My words were coming out so slowly, as if they had frozen up inside me. "Where's Ezekiel?"

Ford set a rag down on the top of an old preaching stand and said what I already knew for sure. "This was going to be a church. The Wheel of Ezekiel Pentecostal Truth Church." He straightened the preaching stand as if he might be getting ready to do some talking.

"Did he sell this place to you?" I must have been shouting, because Ford took a step back.

Then Ford went on talking as if I hadn't just asked him a simple question.

"It had some of the right furniture to make it look like a church, but it still needed the people part of it. I explained that to your sister when she was here." He held up a card. Ezekiel's stained-glass-window card.

Ruth. I needed to find her, but I couldn't make my feet leave.

"Listen, Esther." He slid some boxes of windshield wipers out of the way and sat down on one of the church pews. "I should have told you this when I first met you, but I could never get the right words out. And then the more I got to know you and Ruth, the harder it got, somehow."

I stood in front of him, but I looked at his shoes. Good things always come out easy. People shout them out with barely a second thought. When someone has a hard time choosing the right words, it hardly ever ends up being a good thing he's trying to talk about. And right when my legs were finally starting to take me out of there, Ford reached to the bench behind him and held up a picture.

It was in a nice plastic frame, and it was of me and Ruth. I was wearing the peacock-blue blouse over my pajamas, and it was the year Valley remembered Christmas. That must have been the one and only time I ever wore it, because I don't remember ever seeing it again. Until we opened the Christmas box in the garage. You could see only the edge of his arm, but Ezekiel was in the picture, too, on the other side of Ruth.

I sucked in a sharp breath of air and tried to clear my head. What my mind was trying to tell me couldn't be right, but my heart was telling me it had to be.

And when I finally looked up at Ford, I knew right away why he had that picture and Ezekiel's red Rambler in the barn of his auto-body shop.

I guess I'd never looked all that closely before, but Ford had those Ezekiel streaks of green and gold in his eyes. The same ones I sometimes saw in the mirror when I was brushing my teeth.

My thoughts were bouncing around in my head every which way again, but the only thing I was completely sure of was, I needed to find Ruth.

I turned and headed toward the door. "I have to look for Ruth."

He followed me outside. "She was just here, so she can't be that far." He looked toward the vacant lot. "She took the leftovers of my lunch and a little gardening shovel with a bucket from the shop. She's probably gone on one of your collecting trips without you."

I nodded toward the barn. "If Ezekiel happens by when I'm gone, don't let him leave."

"That's what I've been trying so hard to tell you . . ." he said.

But I was done listening to him right then. I was trying to make myself concentrate hard on Ruth, because I knew I could have easily missed her the first time. And if she hadn't wanted to be found, it wasn't hard to hide that spindly body of hers.

I searched about every inch of the vacant lot. There were so many places for her to hide. I had to lift each piece of wood and look behind each pile. Over an hour had gone by, and I hadn't found even one fallen lick-and-stick star.

My entire body was exhausted. The only good thing was that it would be dark soon. There was no way in the world Ruth would let herself stay outside when the sky got black. But if I didn't find her waiting for me back at home, I didn't know what I was going to do. My mind had stopped making fresh ideas.

As soon as I pushed aside the loose fence board and stepped outside the vacant lot, I saw her. She was plopped down on the grass in the middle of the little graveyard at the side of the road. I wasn't sure it was actually her at first, because we'd always tried to get past cemeteries as fast as possible. Neither one of us had ever even thought about parking ourselves in the middle of one.

If that wasn't strange enough, I thought I could see her chewing on a sandwich. Ford must have known where she was all along, because he sat on the grass next to her, leaning back on his elbows, his legs stretched out in front of him, as if he expected to be there for a while.

I zigzagged through the gravestones to them, trying to stop myself from holding my breath.

Ruth was the type of person that expected everyone to share with her, but she'd never been that good about giving away what she had. But when she held out half a sandwich to me, I wasn't one bit surprised, because she was guilty through and through, and she knew it.

"Peanut butter and raspberry jam," she said in her made-up sugar voice.

I could feel the anger simmering in my stomach when I got close to her, so I turned my face toward Ford instead. "Hey, Ford."

He gave me a quick wave and looked nervously at Ruth.

I narrowed my eyes at Ruth. "I've been looking

all over town for you. You need to follow me home right now." I locked my eyes onto hers. "We've got some things to talk about." Ford and I had quite a bit to talk about, too, but that would have to wait.

Ford sat up and brushed off his elbows. "It is hard to get any work done with Ruth around." But he smiled when he said it, as if he might have liked her company.

"She's been around here for a while, then?" It made me even angrier to think that I had been worrying myself all over the place while she was off collecting and relaxing in the grass eating sandwiches.

He nodded. "Since about lunchtime."

Ruth chewed extra slow and pretended to study something in the grass.

I nudged at her leg with the toe of one of my Keds. "Let's go."

"I'm not done with my dinner." She pointed her sandwich toward the square of marble in the grass beside her. "Ezekiel won't like it if we leave in the middle."

CHAPTER THIRTY-ONE

THE WORDS IN THE MARBLE were carved in tall, wide letters, so I couldn't deny it if I tried.

LEONARD S. BUTLER
1925–1966
LOVING HUSBAND AND FATHER
EZEKIEL 1:3

My head felt as if it had crashing waves in it, and I wasn't sure if my legs were going to hold me up. Ford was beside me, his hand under my arm, lowering me to the grass before I could even start to make sense of everything.

I couldn't catch a whole breath of air. I felt as if someone had gone and punched me as hard as he could. In the up-high part of my stomach, where it hurts the most.

Ford kept his eyes on mine, and those streaks of green and gold in them made my tears come hard and fast.

Ruth and Ford squeezed in on either side of me and waited. The thing was, neither one of them tried to get me to stop, not even Ruth.

"You'll probably cry for a few days or so." Ford said it quietly, because he knew.

Ruth pressed up against me. She never liked it when other people cried. She handed me the napkin from her sandwich, but it had peanut butter all over it, so Ford gave me another one.

"Ezekiel had a deep sickness that got into his lungs." Ford said it slowly and evenly, so we'd pay attention. So I'd pay attention. "The doctor called it cancer of the lungs, but I'd never heard anything like it. He'd get to coughing so hard, I thought his insides were going to come out."

The smell of those cherry cough drops came traveling back to me, and it made my tears slow down to a trickle. "He didn't leave on purpose."

Ford shook his head. "He would never have left on purpose."

I read his name from the square of marble again,

and my breath caught in the very bottom of my own lungs. I remembered all of his coughing. And when he had to be helped up from the couch. "He couldn't be gone," I said. "I found his checks at our house. He couldn't be paying for things if he was gone."

Ford looked up toward the sky as if he was thinking about what to say.

Then Ruth opened up her giant pocketbook and pulled out a narrow handful of papers. She took off the rubber band and handed the stack to Ford. It was a bundle from the bag in Valley's closet. The one with the March note card on top.

Ford went through the pile slowly. Then he fanned it out like a deck of cards and set it all down on the grass in front of him. "Daddy signed these, all right." He picked up one of the checks and touched the date at the top. "But he did it a good seven years ago." He said that last part quietly, as if he was wishing real hard that I was right.

Ruth gathered them up and stuffed everything back in her pocketbook. "What's that mean at the bottom?" She pointed at the *Ezekiel 1:3.*

"It was from his favorite section of the Bible." Ford bent down and ran his hand along the front of the letters. "Ezekiel. That's what everybody called him. He liked the idea that God spoke right to the

Ezekiel in the Bible. Daddy wanted to be special and strong like him."

I closed my eyes tight and tried to pretend I was sitting on one of those church pews in the barn. If I listened real hard, I could almost hear his voice.

Ruth must have been imagining that voice, too, because she opened up that giant pocketbook of hers and pulled out *Charlotte's Web*. She set it on the grass in front of Ezekiel's square of marble.

"Is this it?" Ford picked it up and brushed it off. "The one you were telling me about?"

Ruth nodded, but she wouldn't look at him, and I felt sorry for her, having that crooked streak of Valley in her.

"You might have already figured out something about Ruth." I whispered it to Ford, but I knew Ruth was zeroing in. "She pretty much has the taking part down. But she hasn't quite figured out the giving-back part."

Ford patted me on the arm. "Let's go get my truck, and I'll take you home."

Ruth glanced at Ford over her shoulder and said what I had been wondering for a long while. "How come Ezekiel didn't live with us?"

Ford blew out a long breath of air. "I suppose it was because he already had himself a house."

Ruth squished her forehead together so it made tight wrinkles between her eyebrows. "He lived at your house." She looked back at the tiny house behind us.

Ford nodded. "Daddy never could make up his mind about anything."

"Where's your mom?" Ruth licked at a smear of raspberry jam on the side of her hand. "The one who doesn't much care for Valley?"

I was glad Ruth had thought to ask that question. We didn't need another person nosing around about Valley.

"We moved back to Michigan after Daddy passed. It's where she's from." Ford opened the passenger door of his pickup. Ezekiel's old pickup. "She never did like it here."

"You like it here?" Ruth climbed up onto the seat and scooted over for me.

"I love it," Ford said. "This property is perfect for my car-repair business. Mama had some renters in the house for a while, but she hadn't had anyone in there for a couple of years. When I unpacked my stuff, I really had to air out the rooms."

I looked at the row of shiny silver bumpers to the side of the barn entrance.

"I don't think Mama thought I'd ever come

back here," he said. "She thought it would make me miss Daddy too much." His Ezekiel eyes held steady on mine. "She didn't tell me about you guys until I was packing up to leave Michigan."

I had never thought about someone else missing him. Only Ruth and me. And Ruth didn't know right off that she missed him. I'd had to explain it to her.

"Business has really been picking up the last month or so." He nudged Ruth's foot off the seat and started up the truck.

"I'm helping him hang the new sign." Ruth pointed to a square board next to the bumpers.

Ford smiled to himself in a remembering kind of way. "I'm calling it Ezekiel's Wheel."

I smiled a little, too, because that was the exact name I would've picked.

CHAPTER THIRTY-TWO

FORD HAD NEVER BEEN inside our house before. And when he got out of his pickup, I thought maybe he was just making sure Ruth didn't slam the door like she always does. So I wasn't at all prepared for him to follow us right through the front door. It seemed that he was even harder to stop than Gull when he got his mind wrapped around something. He marched right through to the living room and put his arm out to the side so we couldn't get by.

"Don't you two come any closer." He stood beside the plaster pile and shook his head. "You took out a support wall." He gave a low whistle. "You can't bust out a support wall."

Ruth tried to walk past him anyway, but he took her by the hand and towed her back to the other side of the room. "Is this what you were talking about, Ruth?"

He pointed at the space where the wall used to be. "The popping sound you heard was probably the nails letting go."

He turned to me. "She was going on and on back at the garage about a big hole up to the sky. I thought she was just telling me a story."

"Can you fix it?" I looped my arm through Ruth's elbow.

He leaned his head backward and wrinkled his nose at the ceiling. "I can fix it. But it's going to take some time."

The voice behind me was barely above a whisper. "I didn't mean for anything to happen." Valley had slipped in on her sleepwalking feet, the quiet ones that she has when all the fire has gone out of her.

Aunt Dode doesn't usually have much trouble with her words freezing up, but she stood behind Valley, staring up at the hole, with her mouth wide open and no sound coming out.

Valley took a step toward Ruth, and Ruth pressed into me and wouldn't look at her. Most likely because that ceiling was still fresh in Ruth's mind.

Aunt Dode walked over to us. "She came to my place late last night wanting to borrow money for her remodeling project. Said it was coming out really great, and she'd do my place when she was done here."

I pictured Aunt Dode conjuring up her spirits through a giant hole in her ceiling.

Aunt Dode shook her head. "I said she'd done enough to my place before, and I told her to get lost."

Valley started to cry. A quiet little cry, where the tears move slowly and no sound comes out.

Aunt Dode reached into the front of her shirt and handed Valley a tissue. "Then I found her a little while ago. Curled up under a folding table downstairs at Leona's Sit and Spin." She narrowed her eyes at Valley. "I grabbed her right up and threw her in my car. 'You've got girls to take care of,' I told her. 'You can't be sleeping the day away in a Laundromat.'"

She shook her head at Valley. "There's no way you've got the money for a workman." She nodded toward Ford. "And he's going to charge you for making the trip out here."

But then Ford stared down at Valley with his gold-streaked Ezekiel eyes, and she started crying harder than ever.

Ford didn't say a whole lot of anything, but I knew he was taking in every last word, because he aimed himself toward the kitchen and out the front door.

Then I was the one who felt like crying, because I hadn't even gotten used to having a real brother and Valley had gone and driven him away.

But he was back in a couple of minutes with a black metal toolbox in one hand and a thick note-pad and pencil in the other. He took a silver tape measure out of his toolbox and started writing things down.

Aunt Dode gave Valley an impatient glare, like she wanted to kick her. "I've got to get going. I've got customers." She jerked her thumb toward Ford. "The longer you let him stay, the more he's going to charge. And you're not borrowing it from me."

"A brother wouldn't charge you money, would he?" Ford stood next to me. "I've never given you a bill for what you collected from my lot, have I?" He shook his head, smiling a little, and went back to his measuring.

Aunt Dode's mouth stayed open for a moment, her eyes traveling back and forth from me to Ford. "Well . . . isn't he the spitting image?" Her voice was just above a whisper. "I guess I'll leave you all be, then. I'm sure the four of you have a lot to talk about." She gave me a pat on the shoulder and left.

All of a sudden I was so tired I felt as if I could do like Valley and not come out of my room for about three days.

And Valley's face told me she wanted to go back into her room, where she could block out all the window light, but I think that big pile of ceiling made her stay and listen to me.

"You need to take your pills, Valley." I sat her down right next to that mess of ceiling so she'd have to pay attention.

She nodded and squeezed my arm. But it wasn't an angry kind of squeeze.

Ruth plopped herself down and leaned her head on my shoulder with the Ezekiel picture in her lap. She scraped at a sliver of masking tape with her fingernail.

"Why didn't you tell me, Valley?" It was hard to move Ezekiel to a different part of my mind. The missing part, not the searching part. "Why didn't you tell me he died?"

"I did, Esther. I told the both of you." She tried to take the picture from Ruth, but Ruth clamped her hand over it. "You were both so little, and he was so sick. It was hard to make you understand."

She might have told us that. The words may have been there, but I was having a hard time making myself remember them. It was so much easier to picture him coming back again.

"You dropped us off." Ruth held tightly to the picture and jabbed an accusing elbow at Valley.

I didn't know how Ruth remembered that, but it was true. Valley had left us at Grandma's right after Ezekiel disappeared. I guess, once she started dropping us off, it was hard to get out of the habit.

I pulled out the note from my pouch, but I didn't give it to her. "You've got some things to take care of, Valley." I caught a glimpse of the couch out of the corner of my eye, and I tried to push aside the image that kept trying to form in my mind. The one of Gull's old social worker sitting next to the piles of wall and ceiling dust.

I lowered my voice. "Or someone's going to be dropping Ruth and me off somewhere else. And it won't be Grandma's this time."

It was time for Valley to start paying attention. Ezekiel was gone, but Valley wasn't. I wasn't going to let her escape into her room this time.

It was a good thing that big projects were my specialty, because I had more than a few things to take care of.

CHAPTER THIRTY-THREE

FORD SAYS SOME PEOPLE need more time to get used to life. They can't just go from one thing to the next without a little help. So I made Valley take her pills in front of me every morning, and so far she hadn't given me any trouble. It had been only a couple of weeks, but I'd already noticed a little bit of difference. She seemed quieter somehow. And they made her remember to sleep at nighttime and wake up before breakfast.

I knew Ford was good at fixing cars, but it turned out he was really good at putting walls back, too. His paint job wasn't quite as good as Valley's, but when we got our first look at it, I knew Ruth and I could fix it right up.

"Your friend is outside." Ford sat down at the

kitchen table next to me and handed me a note from his pocket. "She wouldn't let me read it."

I opened it up slowly, and I could almost hear Gull's voice shouting out at me from the paper: "I FOUND NUMBER FIVE!!!!"

Ford lifted one eyebrow at me.

"It's about a book." I got up and went to the door. I smiled when I thought about Gull and Hardy Boys Number Five. I wondered if the librarian had finally broken down and given her the address of the person who had it. It was hard to say no to Gull.

She crouched next to the tree out front, examining my rock garden. I noticed she had a fresh Hardy Boys book sticking out of her coat pocket. One with a cover and without the pages all bent up.

"I'm sorry about wasting your time, Gull." I sat next to her and rearranged some pieces of glass. "Ezekiel's . . ."

"I know." She nodded toward the house. "Ruth told me."

"I guess part of me knew he was gone all along." I was practicing saying in my mind that he had died, but I wasn't quite ready to say it out loud yet.

"You never went to his funeral?" She started to pull out her pen. It was hard for a detective to keep herself from writing things down.

I shook my head. "I'm pretty sure Valley did, though. She took me and Ruth to our grandma's."

Things tend to seem longer when you're four, but I was positive Valley had left us there for a good long while. When she finally came for us, she brought back a mean streak with her. And it hadn't taken us long to notice that that mean streak had glued itself onto her and followed us home.

"What about your grandma? Didn't she ever talk about him dying, either?" Gull scrunched up her forehead.

"I think Grandma just said he was gone." I tried to put myself back to that time. "But I don't actually remember her saying much of anything. For a while after Valley came back for us, Valley would talk about him like he was still around. Like he was going to come walking in at any minute."

Gull nodded.

I watched Ruth come out of the house with Ford. "So, with Valley talking like she was, it wasn't too difficult to do that myself." I took a deep breath.

"But it got harder and harder to even remember what he looked like. So I started telling Ruth about him."

Gull closed her eyes in the deep-thinking way she has. "So she wouldn't forget."

"It's easy to make things up about a person when he's not around," I said.

Ford stood beside his truck, tossing his car keys in the air. "You ready?"

Gull got up and brushed some grass off her pants. "If I'd known you wanted a brother, I could have given you one of mine. Seth and Rollie and Wayne were there for the asking." She tucked her Hardy Boys book under her arm and took off across the grass. "See you later."

Ruth slid over next to Ford, and I climbed in the truck behind her. "I'm ready."

"Is Valley coming?" Ford leaned forward and put the key in the ignition.

I shook my head. "She's out back, sitting in the sun on the Ezekiel couch. Besides, she got to go to the last one. This one's just for us."

When Ford came over, his truck screeched into our driveway, barely stopping before it got to the top. But he always drove carefully with Ruth and me in the car. Today he drove extra slow. Maybe it was to give us all time. Time to remember Ezekiel.

I nudged Ruth with my foot. "Do you know what you're going to say?"

It was so much easier just to say "see you later." Saying good-bye was forever.

Ruth shrugged. "Some of it. I'll probably wait and see what comes to me."

I guess I shouldn't have been surprised that Ruth turned out to be so good at it, with how much she loved the singing and rhythm of the Pentecostals. But when she stood up beside Ezekiel's grave, a genuine preacher's voice came out of her mouth.

"We're here to remember you, Ezekiel." Ruth's voice grew from barely above a whisper to practically a yell and back down again. "We're glad you left Ford, so he can help us remember without making extra stuff up."

I could tell that Ford got a kick out of that one. And I had to smile a little myself. Ruth made it sound as if Ezekiel had dropped Ford down from the sky.

But then Ruth went into "This Little Light of Mine" in a voice so perfect, I was sure it made it all the way up to Ezekiel.

"You want to say anything, Esther?" Ford bent over and fixed a piece of glass on the edge of Ezekiel's rock garden.

I stooped down beside him and took the handful of red china out of my pocket. I'd had to break the Grand Canyon plate, but I knew Ezekiel would understand. It was the only thing that had the exact right color for the Arizona sunset. I arranged it so when the noontime sun hit it you would think you were staring into the real Grand Canyon.

I thought I caught the scent of cherry cough drops when we climbed into Ford's truck.

"I brought you a snack." Ford reached behind the seat and handed us each a foil package. "I thought you might be hungry."

When I unwrapped it, I could feel that the sandwich was still warm. As I took the first bite, I knew Ezekiel would never be completely gone. Because I saw right away that Ford's sandwiches were the perfect kind. The kind where the cheese is all melty and remembers to stay inside.

Many thanks go to the following:

My incredible editor, Reka Simonsen, for always being on the same page and pushing me one step further; my amazing agent at Writers House, Dan Lazar; the hardworking and supportive staff at Henry Holt and Macmillan Children's Publishing Group, including Tim, Caroline, April, and Sarah; Eileen, for being so good at working the books into casual conversation; the Indefatigables, Margaret, Mary Jo, and Pam, who never tire of hearing "just one more draft"; my tri-state critiquers, Bette Anne, Gael, Jame, Laura, Penny, and Shelagh, who will travel miles to read manuscripts and eat good dessert; Pat Giff, for always having time for new writers; Lisa, Chris, and Monique, for keeping my energy up; Denise, Kathleen, Pat, Sue, Linda, Michelle, and all my QH friends, for making the T-shirts, wearing them, and keeping me sane; Dad, for being such a wonderful storyteller, and Lorinda, for holding down the fort; the Village people, weaving up Hickory and down Roseleah, for their untiring friendships and great conversation; Tim and Tom, for almost never making me wish I'd had sisters instead.